MISADVENTURES

WITH A

ROOKIE

BY
TONI ALEO

MISADVENTURES

WITH A
ROOKIE

BY
TONI ALEO

WATERHOUSE PRESS

On the day Misadventures with a Rookie comes out, it will be 1,779 days since I lost my mom. I remember when she was dying; she took my hand and told me to do big things. My mom was the reason I had started reading, and then started writing. She was my biggest fan other than my amazing husband, Michael. Right before my mom had passed, I promised that I would get a book in a bookstore, and her name would be in the dedication.

So, this book is for my mom, Patricia Anne Ortiz. My best friend. My everything. The person I miss more than anything, my mom.

I did it.

CHAPTER ONE

GUS

I'd seen her before.

I'd seen her a bunch of times, actually, since I joined the Malibu Suns a year ago.

But for some reason, this was like seeing her—or better yet, her ass—for the very first time.

Her ass looked like it was from another universe.

As she bent over the ice, her tight gold leggings stretched across her spectacular globes. Craving the chance to slide my fingers along those seductive curves, I could feel my hands shake in my gloves. As I took in her flat stomach and full tits, my cock screamed in the cup I was wearing. I didn't even know her, but I wanted every single inch of her.

When she lifted her head and her eyes met mine, she scrunched her face in an expression of disgust... Distaste? I was pretty sure she knew what I was thinking about, and she didn't look like she liked it one bit. Scooping ice shavings with her shovel, she glared with deep-blue eyes and tossed her blazing red hair over a shoulder. I wanted to look away, but I couldn't. I felt like she was challenging me with her body language, and I was never one to back down from a challenge.

And fuck, it felt tight in my girdle.

I watched her lift her ice-heavy shovel and smack it forcefully against the trash bin. She was probably imagining my head, but all I could focus on was the way her tits strained against that tight little top she and the other ice girls wore. Her stomach muscles were on display, and she was either clenching them or her belly was naturally tight and smooth. This woman... She was what had me gasping for breath, not the thirty-two minutes of ice time I had already played against one of the toughest teams in the American Hockey League.

No, the gorgeous redhead had me gasping in ways I never had before—on or off the ice.

I was a damn good hockey player, the third pick in the first round of the draft. I would've gone first if I had been a little younger and had scored a few more goals—but forty-six points for a defenseman was pretty damn good.

Every pro player wanted to play for the National Hockey League's Twin Cities Tornadoes. They were rebuilding after a horrible year and lots of injuries, so there was opportunity for a player to grow with the team. When they drafted me, I thought I'd made it. I expected to go right in and start playing and training with the Tornadoes, but the owner and general manager had other plans, so they sent me to their farm team first—the Malibu Suns. They said I didn't have enough experience for the big leagues. While I didn't agree at all, my mom always told me, "Keep your head down and work hard, and you'll go places." So I'd been doing just that, even if it felt like I was wasting away in the AHL.

Watching this redheaded beauty was definitely not a

waste of time—though I'd have enjoyed the view a lot more if she hadn't been glaring at me like she could smell my gloves.

"Man, Persson. Did you sleep with her?"

I chuckled, my eyes still on those golden leggings as I shook my head. "Sure didn't. But she doesn't seem to be a fan."

"Bus, I think she killed you six times with those eye daggers of hers." My linemate and closest bud, Max Miller, whistled beside me. "Why the hell are you giving her that look?"

I curved my lips in a grin. "'Cause I'm pretty sure she hates it."

"You're a masochist."

"I am," I joked.

She rolled her eyes, twisted her lips in a scowl of disdain, and skated away.

"Man, she's a she-devil." I grinned, pretty sure I had come out ahead in our silent sparring match.

"With that flaming red hair?" Max grabbed a sport bottle. "Yeah, she probably is."

"I wonder if the carpet matches the drapes." I smirked. I didn't mean to cause my bud to choke on the water he was trying to drink. It was a serious question.

Max laughed when he got over coughing. "Asshole."

"Sorry." I said it, but I wasn't. I seriously did want to know if the carpet matched the drapes. I watched her skate toward the opening in the boards to get off the ice. "Maybe there is no carpet. Those leggings are tight as fuck."

"They don't leave much to the imagination."

"Sure don't," I agreed as I ran my tongue along my lips.

"But I don't think my imagination could come close to the real deal."

Max laughed. "Your imagination might be the only thing that will keep you warm, Bus. 'Cause that girl? She doesn't want anything from you."

"*Yet*," I added confidently as I rolled my shoulders, looking out at the ice. "She just has to get to know me."

When our defensive pairing was called, we cut the conversation and went over the boards with ease. Jumping into the developing play, we skated into the opposition's zone as our forwards rushed the goal. Justine was screening the goalie while Minski and Raddi passed the puck back and forth between each other and back to the points, where Max and I were set up. When the crowd started to get restless, screaming for someone to shoot, Minski shot but missed the goal wide. Thankfully, their defenseman missed the puck, and it slid up the boards and right onto my stick. I circled a bit in my position, watching all the players trying to block me. Finally, I sent the puck to Max. He tried to work it to Raddi, but he was blocked, so once more it came back to me. I took that as a sign that I just needed to shoot. So I did. Hard. I put my whole body into the shot, and when Justine jumped and spread his legs, I knew it was in.

The lamp went off, and I couldn't help but let out a cry of victory as I threw my hands up. Soon the boys were all around, hugging me tightly.

"Atta boy!" Minski yelled.

I smiled, tapping his helmet.

"Let's get this," I yelled back, the roar of the crowd

overwhelming.

I will never get over this. The pure adrenaline that only a crowd can give me. The thrill here was awesome, but still I yearned to play in the NHL. I wanted to be a Tornado. I wanted to play in their arena—the sound effects were fucking intense when a goal was scored. I wanted to play against the teams I had grown up pretending to play against. I wanted to score on the greats. I wanted to slam the same greats into the wall. I wanted—no, I needed—to get there.

And I would.

Gus Persson would fucking make his dreams come true.

I had no doubt about that.

But even after the high of scoring a goal that put us up by three and knowing I was going places, I couldn't shake what Max had said earlier.

Skating beside my buddy, I tried to get back to our earlier conversation. "Why shouldn't I take a shot? She's hot."

Max lifted his brows as he climbed over the boards, and then he scoffed and nodded his head. "Oh, the redhead?"

"Yeah. You said I should stay away from her."

Max rolled his eyes. "I said if I were you I'd stay away. That girl didn't struggle at all with the shovel. All the other girls do. That thing isn't light. But your little redheaded vixen? The one who glared at you the entire time she was cleaning the ice? She had no trouble. She could probably kill you." He looked over at me, laughed, and shook his head. "But you give no fucks and are going to go after her."

I nodded. "Yup. No one says no to me."

"She will."

"No, she won't. She'll love me once I flash these pearly whites at her." I flashed him a wide smile to show him what I meant.

Max laughed. "That she'll know is faker than half the tits on this ice."

I glared. "My teeth aren't fake!"

He gave me a bemused smile. "And I've banged all the Kardashians. It's me. I'm your homie. You don't have to lie."

"They aren't!"

He scoffed. "Whatever you say. But take my advice: Stay away from her. I think she could break you."

I looked over at the ice access door in the boards and grinned. I couldn't see her, but I knew she was there, probably glaring at me.

Why did that make me hard?

"Maybe I like living on the edge."

Max laughed loudly as the whistle was blown. The coach called our defensive pairing. Climbing over the boards, Max said, "There is a difference between living on the edge and running straight for death. That girl is a one-way ticket to Heartbreakville. Or hell. I can't decide. But can I also point out that it annoys me that you can fawn over a girl and still score?"

I laughed out loud as we lined up. "I can score with my eyes closed, Maxy."

"I hate you," he shot back just as the puck was dropped. "And she'll be the only one to block you. I can feel it."

I scoffed. "Well stop feeling things for me and just pay attention to how the game is played. Maybe then you can score."

One of our forwards sent the puck back to me, and I sent it to Max, who shot right away but missed the goal. Raddi got it and tried to score, but his shot was deflected right back to him. He passed it back to Max, who held the puck for a bit while our forwards set up. I saw the tick in his jaw that usually meant he didn't see another play, so when he sent it to me, I was ready.

I shot, and the puck went to the back of the net.

For the third time tonight.

Yes.

Throwing my hands up once more, I looked at Max as he skated toward me shaking his head.

"Show-off."

He was right.

And I didn't take offense at all.

I had been showing off my whole life, and I was ready to show Ms. Redhead all of my wonderful capabilities.

On and off the ice.

CHAPTER TWO

B O

Gus "the Bus" Persson was a showboating, entitled, rich fuck who got on my last nerve. His nickname? Please. *Bus?* He wasn't a bus. He was just a meathead who ran into everyone! I rolled my eyes for the umpteenth time as the fans went nuts, chanting his name and littering the ice with hats following his third goal.

Great. Not only did he ogle me with those sinfully gorgeous green eyes, but I had to clean up after his ass. As the door opened, the girls and I rushed to get the ice clean as fast as we could. In an arena with over fifteen thousand fans and sixty percent of them wearing hats, that wouldn't be as easy as it sounded. With each pile of hats I scooped up, I glared and cursed him as I watched him laughing and high-fiving his teammates.

Ugh, I hated the lot of them.

Especially the rookies. *Grrr.*

They were nothing but trouble. New players were all the same. They went around trying to prove something, fucking everything in their paths before leaving their bedmates in the dark. It was annoying, disgusting, and everything I hated about the sport of hockey. I used to be a fan—a huge fan, actually—when I lived in Minnesota. Not liking hockey wasn't very Minnesotan. Cheering for every hockey team from local high schools up to the pros was a done deal. That was our duty. It was what we did, and I did it well.

Of course, that all changed when I got involved with a player, and boom, things went to utter poo. Nasty poo. But I wasn't that girl anymore. I had moved to California with the drive to succeed as a sports therapist.

Why on earth would I end up back in hockey when I hate hockey players? Well, hockey is what I know. It was really only the antics *off the ice* that sparked my hatred. As a physical therapist, I'd mostly be working with injured players, and they weren't the same at all. They were usually very driven, which I admired. There was a big difference between someone being a showboat—a guy who thought he was hot shit—and someone who was hurt but worked desperately to get back to the sport he loved. I enjoyed being around that type of hockey player, and I sure did love helping them.

Shaking my head, I looked around the arena full of people and bright lights and exhaled hard. When I came to California for physical therapy school, I figured I'd work as a server in some restaurant and wait for my chance to intern, but that wasn't the way the Malibu Physical Therapy program worked. They placed students in internships right away. From day one I received hands-on training, and I loved it. I was especially thrilled when I learned I would be interning with the Malibu Suns, the Twin Cities Tornadoes' farm team.

During my orientation, I learned the Suns were hiring

ice girls. I had done that in Minnesota, so I asked about it. To my surprise, I was hired on the spot. It was insane, but oh so awesome. I was studying a field I loved, had an awesome internship, and was working as both a skating instructor at the practice arena and an ice girl at the games. It was the perfect situation.

The downside was the obnoxious rookies who assumed I was down to fuck. All the time.

Shoveling up another pile of hats, I cursed Gus again. My roommate Lizzy held the trash can. As we stuffed the hats in, she said, "Hopefully this is the only type of score he'll make."

"He's a douche."

Lizzy cracked up at that. "If you'd just give him a little bit, I bet it would be easier for you to chase him off." She paused and looked over at me. "Like you do everyone else."

I scoffed. "Fuck off. I do not chase everyone off."

"You do too," she insisted, shaking her head. "You've been here a year, and no dates, no boyfriends, no nothing. I don't even think you own a dildo."

"Ha. Little do you know, I have six."

"You freak!" she teased.

I beamed at her. Lizzy and I met our first day at MPT. We clicked instantly, and thankfully, she was looking for a roommate. I was living in on-campus housing, but my roommate was disgusting. She would throw dirty panties on the ground and leave them there for a week! Lizzy promised she cleaned, and that was enough to get me to quickly move in with her.

"All you do is work and go to school. We're in our twenties.

We're supposed to be wild and free," she said.

I rolled my eyes. "I have things to do, a future to build. I'll be wild and free in my thirties."

"That's when you're supposed to have kids."

Her words evoked a sharp pang in my heart. By now I was practically a pro at ignoring that pain, so I waved her off, slamming a hat in the bin. "I'll push that back to my forties."

"So you can be sixty when they graduate? Ew, no."

"Hey, I'll be a *hot* sixty-year-old."

She laughed. "You're smoking now, girl!"

Lizzy was insane. All I could do was laugh as I scooped up hats with more force each time. I could hear Gus's voice as he boasted about how easy it was to score on the other team. He was freaking insufferable.

But as much as his ego infuriated me, and as obnoxious as he sounded joking with his teammates, I pictured his moss-green eyes and thick, gorgeous lashes. His rich brown hair was usually stuffed under a helmet, but when he wasn't on the ice, the long layers fell over his eyes. If his full lips and chiseled jaw weren't distracting enough, he had one of the finest bodies I had ever seen. I seriously hated how ripped he was. His sex appeal made me stupid, made me want to touch him. That was *not* going to happen. I knew damn well I needed to keep my distance from Gus Persson.

He was the kind of trouble I had been through, and I wouldn't go through again.

I couldn't.

"Don't worry, he won't be here long. Not with how much he is killing it. He'll be called up to the Tornadoes in no time,"

Lizzy said.

Something else moved in my chest—a different feeling than the sharp pang I felt earlier—but I ignored it and tried to suppress the emotion that threatened to shake my voice. "Good," I sputtered. "I hope he goes. We'll get a break from cleaning up hats."

Lizzy was right. Persson scored hat tricks left and right, which was unheard of for a defenseman. But then again, Persson wasn't your typical defenseman. He could just as easily play forward, but he really dominated on defense. He was a force to be reckoned with. I never understood how he'd gone third in the draft. My dad and I had discussed it for hours. It was insane for a player of his ability to go so late, but he did. The Suns were benefiting from his dominating skill, and eventually the Twin Cities Tornadoes would get the ultimate prize.

Not just Gus Persson...

The Cup.

Maybe?

Men who dominated games and cut down all competition around them used to turn me on. Not anymore. I'd already had a guy like that—someone out to show the world how great he was. Just as the thought crossed my mind, I spotted Gus trying to high-five players on the other team, completely proving my point.

He was just...*ugh*...obnoxious.

Not the kind of guy I wanted anywhere near me.

Nor had time for.

Even if he was sinfully hot.

And sexy.
And talented.
Glaring at him, I shook my head.
Jackass.

CHAPTER THREE

GUS

After every win, the team went to the local sports bar, the Penalty Box. They had the hottest wings and even hotter waitresses. Plus, the owner, Tommy, was a season ticket holder and took good care of the team. After dominating the game, I was ready for some booze, food, and company.

The Penalty Box had all of that.

In abundance.

Walking in behind the guys, I slid my hands along the black tee that hugged my shoulders and chest. I loved this shirt. It was my "getting some puss" shirt. It showed every detail of my chest and then some. Paired with my favorite shorts, there was no chance I'd go home alone tonight.

Not with the ass I had.

I sat down toward the back, near the pool tables and the second bar, and reached for a menu. Max grabbed a seat across from me.

"Why are you looking at that?" He shook his head. "You get the same damn thing every time."

"I do not!"

"You do," he spat back.

I was starting to realize why everyone called us an old married couple. Max was always up my ass, telling me what to do. Yeah, he was older and more experienced, but he wasn't my daddy.

"You're not my dad!"

"Okay, son, relax," he teased.

I glared at him.

"I'm sorry I teased you. Please, look at the menu. Try something else."

I made a face at him as the waitress came to the table. He ordered his regular: wings and a pitcher of beer.

I looked over the menu, scrunching my face up. "Can I get the fish tacos, a grilled cheese with bacon and tomato, and a side of cheese fries? Along with a mug to go with his pitcher?"

Max stared at me as Julie, our regular waitress, just smiled. "So the regular, Bus?"

"Yeah, whatever," I mumbled.

Max laughed while Julie walked away. "I don't know why you fight with me."

"Because you're wrong. All the time."

He scoffed and rolled his eyes. "Come on, I'm ready to kick your ass at pool."

"In your dreams," I called back. "You couldn't beat me if I played with no hands."

"I can, and I will."

"Bring it," I said, swirling chalk at the end of a pool cue. I wasn't one to brag—okay, maybe I was—but there wasn't anything I was bad at. Oh wait, I sucked at knitting. Yeah, I was horrible, and my aunt would tell anyone that. But at everything else, I was awesome.

I looked around the bar, taking in all the females. Most of them I knew and had already slept with. The ones I didn't know, I just wasn't feeling. Probably because I was still thinking about that sexy redheaded ice girl. She was driving me wild. The way she looked at me, like I stole her doll and drew dicks on its mouth, revved my engines. I wanted to kiss the scowl between her eyes, squeeze that naughty ass of hers, and bury my cock deep inside her. And her tits? Man, fucking those would be heaven. It had been a long time since I yearned for a woman, probably because they usually threw themselves at me.

I was pretty sure the only thing redhead wanted to throw at me was a puck.

"Hey, Bus."

It took me a moment to place the voice and the face, but then I remembered her. She was an ice girl, and I had slept with her the first time we met. Shannon? Shanna? Sharron?

"Hey...you," I finally said with a wave. "How you doing?"

"Good. Better if you'd let me take a ride."

Anyone else might have questioned what ride she wanted to take, but I knew good and well. Especially when she opened her legs a bit, her eyes full and lusty as she trailed her fingers up her thighs. Wiggling my finger at her, I called, "Oh now, you know better than that. I don't stick my dick in the honeypot more than once."

She feigned a pout, her lips coming out in a very sexy way. But I had been there, done that, and had the T-shirt. Plus, it wasn't that great.

"Don't you wanna make an exception?" She leaned into her arms, her breasts coming together in a way that almost had me reconsidering. Almost.

"Nope, sweetheart, can't do it. But my boy Maxy can."

Max glared over at me. "I'm getting married."

"Small technicality," I said, waving him off. "Plus, she isn't even here."

"Doesn't mean I don't love her and respect her."

I rolled my eyes. Max was engaged to this girl from back home in Iowa. She was legit a milkmaid, and man, he loved her. She was nice, I guess, but there was no way I would ever be tied down to one girl. That was pathetic. "Whatever. Your loss. Or hers," I said, pointing to Shanna, or whatever her name was.

"Not everyone likes to fuck around like you."

"Why not?" I asked. I stood and struck the cue ball into the racked balls, scattering them around the table. "It's the best of both worlds. Lots of ass and no commitments."

Max rolled his eyes. "I love being committed to one ass."

"Must be a great ass," I teased.

He glared. "You just wait. Your one great ass will come, and then our Gussy Bussy will be tied down forever."

I scoffed at that, pointing my pool stick at him. "The day that happens is the day I don't score."

"I am seriously praying for that day." Maxy stood and took a shot, getting a ball in before looking back up at me. "I'm so tired of having to wait to go to bed."

"Huh?"

"You and the female friends you bring back to the apartment."

I made a face. "No one said you can't go to bed when I have someone over."

He shot me a deadpan look. "No one could sleep when the whole apartment is being filled with 'Oh, harder, Bus, harder. Ugh, ugh, oh, oh, Bus, Bus, Bus—'"

Everyone in earshot started laughing. Hell, even I did as I waved him off. "I get it."

"I swear, it's more obnoxious than you."

I feigned feeling hurt. "How rude."

"You know it's true. And I bet you tell them they need to be loud or you won't give them the full-length Bus."

When he made a crude hand motion, the room was in stitches.

I shook my head. "You're pathetic."

"Takes one to know one," he shot back.

Miller came up and slapped Max's back. "Does he still do that pec thing to music?"

Max laughed, nodding his head. "Every morning." Dropping the stick, he flexed and then started singing "I'm Too Sexy."

"I don't sing that!"

He paused, thinking that over, and then nodded. "That's right, it's usually Beyoncé."

More laughter as I scoffed. "Hey, she's the queen!" The room was loud, and I just smiled as I shot the eight ball in, winning the game. "And like Beyoncé, I slay, motherfucker."

After Julie filled my mug, I took a long swig. Just as I turned to lay my stick against the wall, I found myself toe-to-toe with a certain redhead.

TONI ALEO

She narrowed her eyes as she looked up at me. "Excuse me."

My heart stopped. My eyes widened. My body suddenly felt as hot as her hair. She ducked to walk around me, but I couldn't let her by. Not yet. I stepped in front of her, holding my hands up. "Hey, no need to excuse yourself. Want a beer?"

She shook her head. She was wearing a halter, and her breasts peeked out the sides. Her jeans hugged every inch of her ass. Her long hair was up in a top knot, and her makeup from the game was gone. She looked even hotter without it. Like someone I wanted to wake up to the next morning.

"I'm good," she replied. "I don't drink beer."

I stopped her once again. "I can buy you whatever you want."

Her glare deepened as she shook her head. "No. I'm good."

Once more, I moved to stop her when she tried to walk away. No one turned me down. This was insane. "Hey, what's your name?"

She paused, a smile coming over her face. "My name? That's all you want? Well, it's Fuck Off."

Whoa. What the hell? I didn't understand her hostility. Had I slept with her already? No. No, I hadn't. I'd remember her. As she walked toward her group of friends, I called out, "I don't think you like me."

She turned back, her eyes cutting to mine. "Don't think? Well let me help you with that. No, I don't like you, because I have a tendency to find self-absorbed dicks to be obnoxious assholes."

I held my chest, this time a tad hurt. What a bitch! "Whoa."

"Oh, please don't be surprised. Everyone thinks it; they just won't say it," she added, sitting down and crossing her legs. "But I'm not them."

I could only blink and glance back at Max, whose jaw was almost to the floor. I held my hands out. "What the fuck?"

He looked at me, a grin pulling at his lips. "I don't know, but I love her."

Speechless, I shook my head as I looked back to the redhead who had just cut me in a way no one ever had. Usually women loved me. I'd met a few who didn't, but usually it was because they were playing for the other team! What did I do to this girl?

And why the hell did I want to find out?

Her message was clear—stay the hell away—but I couldn't help it.

I wanted more.

A lot more.

For the simple fact that rejection wasn't really my thing.

CHAPTER FOUR

BO

I hadn't wanted to come out.

I had planned to go home, study, and soak in a nice long bath. I had a heavy schedule tomorrow. I had private classes with clients in the morning, my internship in the afternoon, and my ice skating classes at night. It was going to be a busy day, but Lizzy had convinced me to come out, saying I needed it. I didn't, but since I loved her dearly and didn't want her to think I didn't, I went.

And to my surprise, I was sort of glad I did.

Especially after cutting Gus Persson down to size.

"You've waited a long time to do that, haven't you?" Lizzy asked.

I beamed over at her. "Just a full year."

"Oh, I can tell. You have a slight wiggle to you now."

I laughed. "I just hate how cocky and entitled he is." I rolled my eyes, reaching for my Jack and Coke. "Like I'm supposed to give him my name, or stroke his ego, or let him shove his cock up my ass. Please. I have better things to do, like clean my bathroom."

That had all the girls laughing as we gathered around

the table. There were six ice girls, and while I normally didn't do well in big girl-group settings, I did fine with these girls. Probably because, for the most part, we all had the same goals. Their only drama usually had to deal with the shitty guys they dated. Of course, I didn't date. We all wanted to get through school and make something of ourselves. They tended to sleep with players on the team, but I had bigger plans, and getting distracted by a big doofus of a rookie was not in the cards.

Hell, I didn't have time for anyone, to be honest.

Not even myself.

Which was one of the main points that Lizzy had thrown in my face when she encouraged me to come out.

"Well, Bo, if you were looking for a good time, Persson was your best bet. He's great in bed," Shania informed me. She had slept with him and was begging for another shot.

"He is," Natalie agreed. "So damn good."

"And he's so damn dreamy," Melanie said with a wide grin. "Like so hot. Gah, how do you say no?"

"Easy. No," I said, and she laughed while everyone shook their heads in disbelief.

"He's a one-and-done kind of guy. Great for someone who doesn't want a relationship," Maci said with a saucy grin. "Like you."

I let out a laugh. "I don't care what he does or who he does it with. He is not the guy for me, one time or not. I have more self-respect than to get with a guy who just wants me for sex."

Lizzy shook her head. "You're insane. I'd let him put it in every hole I have."

Everyone sputtered with laughter.

"Even your ear?" Natalie asked.

She nodded, dead serious. "Even my nose."

I gawked at her. "Could you imagine how awful that would be? And then come in your nose?"

That had everyone basically falling over themselves laughing, the whole room filling with our hilarity. Damn, it felt good. So damn good. I just wished it wasn't about Gus Fucking Persson. I rolled my eyes as I leaned back on the bar stool, glancing around the room, but that didn't last before my gaze was trapped by his.

Gus's.

Damn it.

He was staring at me, his eyes so dark, no longer the beautiful green moss that I liked—well, admired. I didn't *like* anything about the guy. His shoulders were back as he leaned into the pool stick he was holding, and his gaze was downright corrupt. It was almost like he was undressing me. Like he didn't care that I'd just told him off. He still wanted to pounce on me, and I didn't understand how that made me feel.

Or better yet, I didn't like how it made me feel.

When his buddy smacked his chest, taking his attention away from me, I thanked the gods above and went back to gossiping with my friends. I couldn't handle his gaze. The more our eyes stayed locked, the more I had to fight the pull that was between us. That was the reason I'd told him off, because I refused to be the girl I *was*—the one I used to be. I refused to go back to the position I came from.

Nope, that wasn't going to happen.

As the night went on, the drinks started flowing, and I was

really glad I'd come out. I already liked the girls, but getting to know them outside of school and work was awesome. We were all cut from the same cloth, and I liked that.

"I lived in a trailer," Lizzy said with a laugh. "I was straight trailer trash, but then my mom married this movie producer, and all of a sudden, we were rich. It was insane."

"No way!" Maci yelled. "You're rich?"

She scoffed. "My stepdad is. I mean, he spoils me and pays for my apartment, but I'm not rich."

I reached over and grabbed her shoulder with my hand. "Your dad pays for the apartment?"

She grinned. "He pays my half."

"And you couldn't get him to pay mine?"

"He does."

I glared at her.

"Sometimes," she admitted, "I revert back to my trailer park ways and pocket the money."

We all laughed, and I glared again. "That is rude."

"I know. I'm sorry. You understand, right? You're a fellow trailer parker."

I laughed as I shook my head. "Actually, I grew up blue collar. I had to work for everything I wanted, and because of it, I wanted big things."

"I can tell," she said with a grim smile. "You aren't mad, are you?"

"Nah, I pay my way, and if that helps you out, that's awesome."

She let out a breath. "You're the best. And to think, guys, we could have lost her to Stanford."

Everyone gasped and looked at me.

"Huh? Really? You chose MPT over Stanford?" Shania asked, her brows pulled together. "Are you crazy?"

I waved her off. "I had plans to go to Stanford to be a doctor, but—" I stopped short, blinking a few times. Man, I was a tad drunk. How had I almost said that? *Shit.* "I didn't get in, and boom, I'm going to school for PT." I waved my hands in the air for emphasis, and thankfully everyone laughed at me.

Well, except Lizzy, who was looking at me with a certain look in her eyes. A look, I was finding, I did not like. "You're lying to us."

I pressed my hands into my chest. "Me? Never."

"Yes! You did get in, didn't you?"

"No, I didn't," I lied even more, and I hated lying. It wasn't my strong suit, and I could tell by the way Lizzy was looking at me that I wasn't doing well. Nope, she was onto me, and the more time that passed, the more everyone else was eyeing me.

"You are lying!" Maci called out. "What? Did you not go for a guy?"

I scoffed at that. "No. No dude would hold me back from my dreams like that. It wasn't that. Really, I didn't get in."

"No, you did. You're smart. Like, übersmart. Isn't she the top of the class?" Shania asked, and everyone nodded. "Yeah, way too smart for our little PT school."

"Hey, I love our PT school."

"We do too," Lizzy said, but then she held her finger out, pointing it at me. "But I also know you would've gone to Stanford if you could have, so spill it. Everyone else has, so you have to also."

I started to sputter, unsure what to say, because there was no way I would admit why I didn't go to Stanford. Everyone's eyes were on me. I felt my skin prickle with sweat, and I wanted to run. I hadn't told anyone why I moved here. Why I ran away from home and from my dream of being a doctor. I couldn't. My secrets were embarrassing and pitiful.

I was a pathetic excuse for a human being according to some people—especially my parents.

Before I could try another lie, we were interrupted. "Listen..."

My anxiety went through the roof. I was panicking under the stress of the conversation, the emotions of what I'd been through and what I was trying to move past, and when my gaze met his, I couldn't breathe. "You."

He waved awkwardly, and for the first time, Gus looked unsure of himself. That moment of vulnerability on his strong features was sort of hot. "Yeah, me."

He was so close, only inches away, and I swore I could feel the heat from his large body. Before he could go on, I was off my bar stool, pushing it between us. "What do you want?"

"I want to talk to you. I feel like we've gotten off on the wrong foot."

I laughed but without humor, a nervous tone in my voice. "We haven't gotten off on any foot. There is no need for a foot. I don't want anything to do with you."

He paused, and I heard some of the girls gasp behind me. Apparently these girls never rejected Gus. Well, I wasn't like them, and I was pretty sure I made that clear.

"See," he said. "I don't understand that. Please, explain."

I glared. Usually, I'd walk away. Especially since I don't have to explain myself to anyone. But I guess the alcohol and anxiety were burning hot in my veins, because soon I was leaning on the chair, holding his gaze. "I don't have to explain anything to you. You're nothing to me."

He pointed to me. "See? What is that hostility?"

I glared. "There is none." Well, of course there was. "I don't want to talk to you, but since I'm pretty sure you won't leave me alone—"

"Oh, good. This is killing me, and the fact that I don't know your name is really bothering me. So please spill."

"Can I speak?"

He nodded, his eyes narrowed. "Go right ahead, but tell me your name first. And are you from Minnesota? You have that very Minnesota tone."

The girls giggled behind me. I was pretty sure he was making fun of my accent.

Asshole.

"I'll never tell you my name, and that's that," I snapped, shaking my head. "And what makes you think I'm from Minnesota?"

He grinned, his teeth so white and so straight. Probably fake. "The way you say Minnesoooota."

I glared, and he kept on grinning.

"So why don't we just add your name in there, and we can be on good terms?"

"We will never be on good terms."

"We will."

"Never," I grated. "Because I don't want anything to do

with you. You are not the kind of guy I want to be around."

"You don't even know me!" The look on his face, one that probably meant he was serious, had me laughing.

"Oh, I know you fine and well," I decided.

"You do not."

"I do too!" I hollered back, and yes, I realized we sounded like two kids, but I didn't care. "Just go away."

"No, you claim to know me," he said, his voice stern. He got closer, leaning into the bar, his face right in line with mine. So close I could see the stubble on his jaw and a little cut along his lip that was new and fresh. I wanted to touch it. I wasn't sure why, probably because I was drunk, but soon I forgot all about that as he whispered, "So tell me, redhead, who am I?"

"Who are you?" I asked, my eyes darkening as I leaned in.

"Well, let me tell you."

CHAPTER FIVE

GUS

Redhead's eyes were blazing blue. So bright, almost like crystals, as she glared back at me. She was fire hot, and fuck, I wanted to kiss that pouty mouth of hers. Or even the space between her eyes that was full of angry wrinkles but so damn hot. She looked so annoyed, and I must say, I was really digging the splotches of color along her face. I wondered if they were all over her. I liked how she looked at me. I bet she really thought she was acting out of anger or even hatred, but I knew it was out of lust. I just needed to make her realize it.

And then, right to bed we'd go.

But before that could happen, she obviously had something to say. Her lips were trembling and her body was shaking as she glared up at me. I wanted to laugh, I did, but I was pretty sure she would hit me.

I wasn't sure if I wanted that or not...

"Bet you grew up in one of those big fancy houses with the built-in rink in the back yard that your daddy spent hours on. I bet you had a car by fifteen—and not some beater car. You had a Camaro or, better yet, a Lexus. You never had to beg for a girl's attention, ever. You had the girls doing your homework every day, and the teacher's assistant made sure you got the answer key so you could memorize it." She paused, her eyes full of fire.

I couldn't disagree with her. She was hitting every nail on the head. With more force than I expected.

"You were idolized as a kid. The star player. Everyone loved you. You were treated like a god, and you let it go to your head because why wouldn't you? Everyone loved you, everyone wanted to have sex with you because you're Gus Persson, and everyone wanted a piece. Then you come here, again the star, even if you think you should have gone straight to the Tornadoes. So to make sure everyone knew they made a mistake, you start playing super hard here, just to keep the idolization going. You're obnoxious so people see you, hear you. Because you love the attention. You yearn for it. But I'm here to tell you, Gus Persson, you'll never get it from me. Ever."

Swallowing hard, I kept my eyes on her, and soon I realized we were both breathing hard. Her little speech hit home on many levels. Maybe she did know me, and I wasn't sure how that made me feel. No, I did... It turned me the fuck on. The way her breasts were rising and falling with each breath, the wild in her eyes, and those lips in that pout—it was deadly. I wanted to kiss her. I wanted to touch her. Fuck, I wanted her, but to keep from doing that, I crossed my arms, clicking my tongue as I held her gaze. "You got me all figured out, huh?"

"Yes," she somehow got out before taking a step back, probably thinking the distance would halt what was brewing between us. "And I know all you want is to fuck me and nothing else. I won't be another little mark on your hockey stick, big boy. I deserve more than that."

The girls behind her all looked away, embarrassed. I could hear my friends laughing and razzing me, but I didn't care. Nothing mattered at that moment but her. I didn't even know her name—didn't know anything, really—but I wanted to know it all. And then some. If she thought I didn't see her reinforce herself against the table to keep from falling over, I did, and that meant one thing.

I affected her.

I didn't have to be obnoxious or cocky to see that.

With a tip of my lips, I asked, "So now it's my turn, right?"

Her brows came in, her eyes darkening as she looked up at me. "Huh?"

"My turn," I said once more, this time pressing my elbows into the chair so that we were eye-to-eye. "I bet you are super smart, one of those girls who fights for female rights, but not like the real feminists. Like a wannabe one. You make sure to shave and make sure you smell right. I bet you never share anything on Facebook about 'the fight for women' because you don't want the attention. You want to fly under the radar and keep everyone away. You were more than likely hurt by someone who you assume is just like me. Do I look like him? Is that the problem? Did he dump you for the cheerleader because you were too smart?"

"Fuck you," she sneered.

I beamed. "We'll get there," I say. "See, the thing is, No Name Nancy, it doesn't matter, because no matter how much you say you don't like me because of my upbringing or my amazing skills on the ice or even because I look like the dude who fucked you over—you do like me. A lot. You think about me more than you should. You yearn for my touch because you want to know what it feels like. You don't want to. You hate it, which in turn makes you hate me. But sweetheart, that doesn't mean you shouldn't let me touch you."

I reached out, trying to cup her shoulders, but she moved. "Over my dead body."

That makes me laugh. "See, more of that 'I have to say no to keep my word,' when really, all you want to do is scream yes while I'm deep inside you."

Her eyes widened, but she didn't seem shocked as she pushed the stool away, making me stand so that she could go toe-to-toe with me. With a tip of her chin, her eyes ever so dark, she mocked, "Then take me."

Huh? "What?"

"Take me, right here, if I want it. Take it. Fuck me against every surface in this bar. Show me how much I want it," she demanded, her eyes sparkling with the challenge. Wow, what a turn of events we had here.

But I wasn't that stupid.

"So you can kick me in the junk and claim assault? Yeah, right. I haven't been hit in the head that many times, honey." I moved in closer. Fuck, I think the world might have stopped when she took in a breath.

Gasping a bit, she looked up at me. "I wouldn't. I'm asking for it."

"So you're telling me you are?"

She took in another breath, her chin high and challenge in her eyes. She was convinced I wouldn't do it. "I am 'cause I know you won't do it."

"I won't?" I asked, my voice husky and all kinds of wrong. My whole body was burning, and I wanted more than anything to do what she asked, but I couldn't. Not yet. "How do you know?"

"Because I bet you can't even get it up. You'd probably break under the pressure of everyone seeing."

Oh, she was funny. Laughing, I shook my head. "I never snap under pressure. Ever."

"Says the guy who is just standing there, staring at me."

"I don't even know your name. I like to know a lady's name before I fuck her."

That surprised her but only for a second before her swag came back. "You do? I never would have suspected that. But I did suspect you'd do nothing, because you aren't the guy you want everyone to believe you are. You want the attention, you thrive off it, but when it comes to a woman who could actually challenge you, you snap like a twig. You aren't made for the real connection. You're made for the fake fuck. And until you figure that out, you'll be alone and pathetic, fucking everyone you see."

Wow. Why did that annoy me? "You don't know shit."

She feigned innocence. "I don't?"

She was driving me insane, and before I could think or stop myself, I took her face in my hands. She smelled like heaven, and I felt like I was at the pearly gates right as my lips touched hers. They were so thick, like honey, and tasted just as sweet. I could hear commotion around us, but then I couldn't. I was too focused on her lips and the feel of her sweet cheeks against my hands. It was mind-blowing. I wasn't one to assume a kiss could rock my world, but then again, according to this chick, I was going to be alone for the rest of my life.

The kiss was over before it could really get started as she whipped back, her eyes wide as she yelled, "How dare you!"

With a smug grin, I said, "You said I wouldn't. Guess you were wrong."

Flabbergasted, she backed away, and when she started to shake her fist, I had to hold back my laughter. "I said you wouldn't fuck me against every surface! So I wasn't wrong because you didn't."

I held my finger up. "No, you said take what I want, and I wanted your mouth on mine. I got it."

"You son of a bitch."

I grinned. "Actually, my mom is really nice. She'd love you." With a wink, I was rewarded with a frustrated scream that had my groin tight. "And don't worry, I'll get you to tell me your name. So I can scream it."

Our eyes stayed locked for another second before I winked once more and then turned around slowly, clapping my hands as I met Max's wide gaze.

"Maxy, ready for another round?"

I glanced back at her and saw her hands were shaking. She looked like she was going to attack me, and all I could do was grin.

And she thought she was going to put me in my place.

Hah.

CHAPTER SIX

B O

"That cocky son of a bitch."

"Um, did anyone else see the fireworks?" Lizzy asked, her eyes wide and full of all things gooey and sweet. Like how they always got when we would watch a stupid romance movie. She loved that shit, but I'd be damned if she put that fake shit on me. That was not my jam.

But before I could even mutter anything, Maci squealed, "Yes! Oh my goodness! They are so into each other."

"I'm right here," I complained, but obviously no one was listening.

"Did you see the way he looked at her?" Natalie asked. "It was so hot. So hot. And oh my God, I'm hot everywhere."

"For fuck's sake," I mumbled as Lizzy pointed to Natalie.

"Right? I mean, holy moly. Bo, tell me you didn't feel that?"

I looked her dead in the face. "I felt nothing but my hate fire growing fast and hot."

"Right! I'm hot too!"

For the love of God. I was getting nowhere with these people. All I felt was my growing anger toward Gus. How dare he! He didn't know me! He was delusional, and how dare he say those things! He basically made me out to be some smart girl who fluttered around, acting dumb. That wasn't me. He and his stupid antics could go right to hell!

And that kiss?

Argh! Oh, how he used my words against me. That son of a bitch! Even if he did taste like everything right and wrong in the world. Or that his lips took mine in a way I had never experienced before. Because, damn it, I didn't want to experience it!

Damn it!

Stewing, I leaned back in my seat and crossed my arms over my chest as the girls went on and on about how fucking hot Gus Persson was. I bet he was watching, loving every second of it. He strived for this kind of attention. It was all a ploy, another way to get all the attention. He was so pathetic, and I wished he would just go away. But he wouldn't, not anytime soon. Which was annoying as hell.

Ugh.

When his laughter filled the room—the obnoxious sound sending chills down my spine—my gaze cut to where he was leaning on the pool table. His whole body was moving with the motion of his laughter. Glaring, I watched as he leaned into his pool stick, his jaw slack as the guy in front of him said something that was apparently very funny. Looking at his dark hair and thick jaw, I wanted to say he looked like Jesse, the guy who had fucked me over, just like Gus had said. But he didn't look like Jesse. Jesse had soft features and wasn't that big. Gus took up the whole room. He was so big, so handsome, and fuck, yeah, maybe he did do something to my insides, but I'd never act on it. Not even in my drunken state.

It was just a simple movement, his gaze casually meeting mine. My skin was prickling, and it wasn't from a draft. Gone was the smug look and even the cockiness. All that was left was a dark and smoldering look in his eyes as he held my gaze. His shoulders went back, his tongue coming out to wet his lips, and within seconds I could feel that tongue on mine. It was quick, maybe just half a second, but I would never forget it.

Leaning on his pool stick, he took in a deep breath, filling his wide chest before blowing it out, his gaze never leaving mine. Heat gathered between my legs, and soon I was squirming in my seat, but I wouldn't look away. I wouldn't let him win.

But he must have seen my struggle, because within seconds, back came that stupid cocky grin, and then he blew me a kiss.

"Motherfu..." My words trailed off as I looked away, mad that I'd allowed him to hold my gaze for that long. What the hell was wrong with me? Was I really that drunk? I reached for my purse, but Lizzy stopped me.

"No, don't leave!"

I rolled my eyes. "I'm not. I'm going to the bar for a drink."

"We can order them."

My gaze went back to where he was watching me, and I shook my head. "I need some space."

And I wasn't lying. Plus, I planned to get some water and didn't want her to see. I did not like the person I was becoming with each swig of my drink. Nope, that girl was dumb, and I refused to not be level-headed right now or lose control. Not with Gus in the room.

Even if I wanted so desperately to do so.

Ugh. Why had I thought that?

Shaking my head in disgust, I left the room and entered the next. It was busy, so it took me a moment to get to the bar. When I reached it, I leaned on it before waving to the bartender. He saw me, flashed me one finger that I assumed meant one second. Letting out a breath, I leaned on my elbows and pulled out my phone. Hitting Facebook, I scrolled through my feed as I waited. When Gus's earlier words came into my head, I rolled my eyes. He didn't know anything about me. I shared all kinds of stuff that I believed in—but, oh my God, *why did I care*?

He was an asshole anyway.

When a picture my mom had posted appeared, I smiled. Davis's toothless grin took up the whole screen. He was so adorable and getting so big. I hated that I was missing this time with him. But I'd decided that was what I wanted when I left home. Conflicting emotions clogged my throat as I took in his dark-red hair and light-blue eyes. Closing my eyes, I cursed the stupid alcohol I had consumed.

New rule: no more drinking.

Apparently, I turned into a complete sappy idiot.

"Cute kid."

My eyes shot open at his voice. When I looked over and realized that Gus was way too close for my liking, I tried to step back, but someone was behind me. Since I'm pretty sure the dude behind me didn't want me on top of him, I was stuck. I didn't want to lose my place at the bar, so I stayed where I was. Even if I could feel every inch of him. Swallowing hard, I hit the home screen on my phone so the picture would go away.

"Thanks," I said brusquely.

"Yours?"

My heart stopped, and I slowly shook my head. "No."

"Brother?"

"Yeah," I answered, but I wasn't sure why I was answering him.

"I thought you were too young to have a kid."

I shrugged.

He laughed. "I'm surprised you're talking to me."

I nodded. "Me too."

He chuckled as he leaned into the bar beside me, holding up a finger. Apparently, Gus had magic fingers, because the bartender appeared right away. "Bus, what's up? What can I get you?"

"Another beer for me and my friend here."

I shook my head. "Just a water, please, and my tab."

The bartender nodded before going to work, and I could feel Gus's gaze on me before he said, "Done drinking for the night?"

"Yeah, I turn into an idiot when I drink."

"Oh?"

"Yeah, I argue with irresponsible and pigheaded people."

He scoffed. "I'm guessing I'm the irresponsible and pigheaded people you speak of?"

"Yup," I answered simply. Out of the corner of my eye, I saw that stupid grin of his. Looking over at him, I was once again hit with his good looks, and instantly, I was annoyed. Why was he so beautiful? It was honestly unfair, especially considering how talented he was. "The one and only, actually. I should correct that sentence to person."

"Well, I'm sorry you feel that way."

I scoffed. "You are not. You couldn't care less."

"I do, actually," he said simply, his eyes burning into mine. "I still feel we've gotten off on the wrong foot."

"Again, no foot needed," I said as my water, tab, card, and ID were laid on the counter. "We don't have anything to say to each other."

He moved closer to me, but I ignored him as I signed my tab.

"Actually, we have a lot to say— Holy shit, is your name really Bocephus?"

My stomach dropped as I realized he wasn't getting close enough to me to make me nervous but to see my name! "You sly asshole!" I yelled, tucking my ID and card into my pocket. "You weren't supposed to see that."

"I wouldn't want anyone to see that either. No wonder you wouldn't tell me your name!"

"Oh, shut up!"

His eyes were wild. In another world, I'd say he was adorable.

"Bocephus? As in Hank Williams Jr.? That's just cruel."

"It's not a big deal."

"Jesus, do your parents even love you?"

I glared. "Shut up. They do! They're big fans."

His eyes widened, and his shock was actually charming.

"So, my parents are big Mötley Crüe fans, but my name isn't Mötley!"

"Like Gus is any better!"

He feigned hurt. "Hey, Gus is a man's name. A strong name. Plus, it rhymes with Bus, which works well for my career."

I pursed my lips in aggravation. "So you're telling me your parents wanted to call you Gus 'cause they knew you'd play hockey and you'd be the *Bus*?"

He curved his lips and slowly shook his head. "No, actually, my name is August, but my mom has called me Gus since I was a baby. It stuck."

It was obvious he loved his mom. His cheeks reddened a bit, and his lips turned up in such an innocent way. Watching his face, I couldn't help but think he looked like an August. Which knocked me right back into reality. He was the rich kid I was supposed to hate! He was probably carrying all his daddy's credit cards and all his bills were being paid on time, but not by him. Shit, all he was missing with that stupid tight shirt and even tighter shorts was his silver spoon.

"Awesome. Information I'll never need to know again." Pushing the tab forward, I took a long swig of my water and then set it down. "Yeah. So this was fun—not."

I went to turn but his arm came around my waist and he pulled me against his chest, hard with muscle. His hips pressed against the small of my back, and I swore my pussy came to attention. Breathless, I closed my eyes as his lips grazed my ear.

"But when I do see you again, should I call you Bocephus?

Or do you go by something else?"

Swallowing hard, I struggled against him, but his grip was ironclad. If I was honest, I wasn't fighting that hard. I loved the feel of him against me. The way his thighs pressed into my ass and how I swore I could feel the length of him. Tomorrow, I would be angry with myself that I allowed him to touch me like this. But tonight, I'd let it happen for a second more.

His lips pressed into my ear. "What's your middle name? Surely, you go by that."

His laughter had my skin breaking into gooseflesh as I gasped for breath, and when I stepped forward to put some space between us, he took ahold of my hand, lacing his fingers with mine. My gaze moved from our entangled hands to his gaze. His green eyes were dark, like emeralds, and everything went blazing hot.

"Maybe I go by Bocephus."

He laughed, shaking his head. "No, you don't, and even if you do, I don't think I can moan that without laughing extremely hard afterwards."

He wasn't funny. He wasn't, yet I found myself fighting back my laughter as I looked away, my hand on fire in his. Swallowing hard, I looked up and shrugged. "I think it would be hot."

That had him laughing more as he pulled me closer to him, and I found myself not fighting him. I wasn't even drinking. How was I getting even more drunk? What the hell was wrong with me?

"Give me something to call you."

I shook my head. "No reason to."

"Sure there is."

"Give me one good reason," I demanded.

"So when I see you, I don't have to call out 'Howdy, Bocephus!'"

I rolled my eyes. I didn't want him doing that since no one knew my real name, so I shrugged. "It's Bo."

"Bo?"

I nodded. "Yeah, when I was younger, I went by Bo Jane. BJ for short."

His eyes lit up. "So what you're really telling me is that you're amazing at BJs?"

My smile dropped, and I pulled my hand away. "And I'm out."

"Wait!" he called, taking my hand once more, but I pulled it away as he followed me through the bar. "Let me take you out."

"Drop dead."

He laughed. "You say no, but I know you mean yes!"

"I hope you die slowly."

His laughter followed me out and into the easy breeze that I had started to love more and more since moving to California. As I pulled out my phone to request an Uber, he came up beside me.

"Are you really gonna blow me off?" he asked.

"Sure am."

"But we were getting along so well."

"Go step on a Lego, please."

He laughed. "I think we'd have fun."

"If I wanted fun, I'd fuck someone else. Promise."

He made a face. "So you're telling me you're not attracted to me at all."

"Exactly. Not even in the slightest."

He just laughed. Hard. "Liar. Everyone is attracted to me."

I didn't react as I requested the Uber and then opened my Facebook. "Well, I am not everyone."

"I am seeing that. How can I get you to admit you want me?"

"Won't happen. Go on, we're done."

Out of the corner of my eye, I could see that he had crossed his arms over his chest. He leaned close to me, and I could feel his lips against my cheek as he whispered, "Oh, Bo Jane, we are far from done."

I closed my eyes and inhaled sharply. I hoped he'd go away, but then his lips pressed into my cheek, and I jerked my head away. Meeting his gaze, I glared, but he just grinned in the easygoing and confident way that had my blood boiling.

"Till next time." He smirked.

"There will be no next time."

His eyes sparkled with certainty. "Yes, there will be."

I rolled my eyes. "I'm telling you. There won't."

"There will," he called, and when I went to disagree, I saw that he had closed the bar door with a slam. Biting my lip, I looked back at my phone, my skin crawling. I would be lying if I said I wasn't a little scared by the confidence in his voice.

No, it didn't matter.

Nothing was going to happen between us.

Right?

CHAPTER SEVEN

BO

His mouth felt like a rose running between my breasts, taking my breath.

His rough, calloused hands held my hips as he trailed kisses down my stomach and dipped his tongue in my belly button as I arched up against his mouth. My pussy was throbbing, dripping wet from his slow torture. He hadn't shaved, and his jaw was rough with hair as he dragged it along my skin. It did nothing but drive me crazy. Every single inch of my body was on fire.

Everywhere.

I hadn't been touched by a man in a while. I hadn't yearned for a man until now, and as he fell between my legs, I could do nothing but whimper. Slowly, his tongue made circles around my belly button before running down to my mound, where his chin was tickling my lips. His shoulders were thick with muscle I dug into with my nails. I arched up, wanting his mouth on me.

Needing it.

Slowly spreading me apart, his elbows dug into my knees as he chuckled against my center. "Jesus, you're dripping for me."

I couldn't speak, nor did he wait for me to, before dipping his tongue between my swollen lips—and I swear I couldn't hear anything but my heartbeat. I cried out as he slowly dragged his finger along me, dipping deep inside me. I couldn't catch my breath. Gasping as he circled his tongue along my clit, I tried to arch more, but his hand sprawled across my stomach, holding me down as his tongue and fingers tortured me.

Sucking my bud between his lips, he flicked his tongue, making me squirm and whimper even louder. The sounds coming from me were like none I had ever heard in my life. They were somewhere between pure pleasure and absolute need. He was making me crazy, but I didn't want him to stop.

"Please don't stop," I cried out. He sucked my lips and my clit into his mouth. The pressure was unreal, and soon I was shaking and screaming with my release, my whole body jerking against his mouth. I held his head right where I wanted it.

Where I needed it.

And boy, he didn't hold back. Sucking my clit as I rode my orgasm, he was relentless, his fingers biting into my thighs. I cried out, thrashing against his mouth. Taking me by the backs of my knees, he pushed my legs back until they touched the bed as he fucked me with his tongue, my cries filling the room as he swallowed me whole. When he stopped, I thought he was done, but he wasn't.

Soon his cock was deep inside me.

So big.

So thick.

And fuck, why did he fill me so completely? Perfectly. I swear I could feel him in my chest as he pounded into me. I looked up at him. He was so gorgeous, his chest so thick and wide. His abs clenched, sweat dripping down his body as he slammed into me, our bodies making the most beautiful music I had ever heard.

"I swear, you're the hottest woman I have ever seen."

Holding the top of the bed, I tipped my hips up so he could go deeper, both of us moaning with the simple movement. "You're going to break me."

"You're fucking right I am," he grunted as he thrust deeper and with more force. "Your heart, your body. Everything. I will break you. Hurt you. I'm not good enough for you."

"I know. I don't care. Fuck me," I cried out, arching, my body squeezing his as my toes curled. But then he pulled out of me, flipped me on my stomach, and brought my hips up before entering me from behind, his cock going deeper than before. "Oh, fuck."

"That's right," he murmured against my back, jackhammering hard into me. My ass smacked into his thighs with each thrust. Holding on to the sheet, I cried into him, his body so deep inside mine as another orgasm started to build. I couldn't believe it. I was about to come again, and that would be a first. He was so fucking big, he hit all the right places. I couldn't fathom it. I hated this guy, but man, he fucked like a dream.

When my head jerked back, his fingers tangled in my hair, I hissed out a breath as his lips came to my cheeks, trailing kisses along them.

"Stay away from me. I'll ruin you," he grunted against my ear.

"Fuck, oh fuck, Gus, fuck me harder."

"Oh, I will, and you're going to love it."

"I know, fuck, yes!" I screamed, squeezing him with my pussy, my legs tangled with his as his grip on my hair tightened. When I started to come, my whole body went taut. He continued slamming into me as I cried out. He grazed my jaw with his teeth, and I squeezed my eyes shut.

"You'll never feel this again," he whispered against my hair, still fucking me, his cock throbbing inside me. "I'm it. Give in to me. Give it all to me."

"I am," I cried, leaning my head back against his shoulder as his lips took mine, his tongue moving into my mouth in a kiss so sloppy but also so fucking hot. Pulling away, he bit into my bottom lip before I wailed out, "I'm yours."

"That's fucking right. All mine," he demanded before he slammed into me once more, our bodies stilling as he filled me, twitching against me as he came. His body felt so hard against mine as he trapped me in his arms and rolled over so that my back was against his chest. Gasping for breath, he trailed his lips along the back of my head as he whispered, "I'm gonna fuck you all night."

I couldn't say anything but "Okay."

"And you're not going to stop me."

"I'm not."

"Because you want me."

"I do."

"You love me. You do. You just don't want to."

Jerking awake, I sat up quickly, and the motion had me gagging. Covering my mouth, I swallowed back the bile as my eyes adjusted to my dark room. Looking around, I inhaled through my nose as my heart jackhammered in my chest. I looked around my bed, and thank sweet baby Jesus, it was empty.

"Fucking hell."

That dream was so vivid. It felt so damn real, my pussy was still throbbing. But that wasn't what scared the hell out of me. No, it wasn't even that I was fucking Gus Persson. It was what he had said. Love him? That was insane. I wouldn't. I couldn't. Ever. It was a joke. My dream was playing a joke on me.

But fucking fuck, it felt so damn real...

CHAPTER EIGHT

BO

"Liz, have you seen my bank card?"

Throwing things around, looking for my bank card, I let out a long breath. My head was pounding, I had dry mouth like crazy, and I was so sexually frustrated I was sure I was going to snap in half. I tried to get a release last night, but every time I tried, Gus's stupid face came into view, and back came the dream. Nasty cycle. I didn't understand it. I didn't like him, not even a little bit. He was everything I hated and more. Yet, I couldn't stop thinking about him, and all I wanted was his lips on mine once more. I wanted to press myself up against him. Feel his length against my swollen pussy, and fuck, I wanted him between my legs. As long as he didn't open his mouth, I could ride him for hours.

Oh my God, I was becoming like the other girls! After one night, I was under that stupid, cocky asshole's spell! How in the world! I was not that pathetic. But then, what if I did just give in? One night and done. He was known for that. No, I wasn't that person! I was better than that. But damn it, I wanted him. As if I didn't have enough to worry about. Why was my life so hard?

No one to blame but myself.

"Where the hell is my card!"

I grabbed the jeans I wore the night before and shook them as Lizzy, looking like a hot, tired mess, stumbled out of her room and leaned into my doorway. "Can you stop yelling? I feel like death."

"You look it too," I snapped back at her as I tore my purse open again.

"Wow. Thanks."

"Dude, this isn't funny. I need my card. Fuck me," I groaned, almost in tears. This wasn't me. I was very good about keeping up with my stuff. But no, I went to a bar, I drank, and ladies and gentlemen, prepare yourselves to meet idiot Bo.

"Did you call the Penalty Box?"

I hadn't. I picked up my phone and dialed, tapping my foot on the ground as I checked the time. I didn't have much time to get to the rink for my lessons, which meant I could kiss eating breakfast goodbye. When the waitress answered, she informed me that my card hadn't been turned in.

Letting my hand fall to my thigh, I groaned loudly. "No, it's not there."

"I'm sure it's in here somewhere. I'll keep looking. Go to work," Lizzy said as she slowly fell into the couch, burying her face in the pillow.

"Please look for me. I'm about to be late."

She waved me off, nodding her head. "I promise I will look as soon as my head stops pounding."

I wanted to cry, but I had no choice but to agree and rush out the door.

Ugh, it was going to be a long fucking day.

◆ ◆ ◆ ◆

I wanted to say I was one of those really great coaches that left everything at the door and taught my kids, but unfortunately I couldn't say that. I coached to the best of my abilities, but my mind kept going back to where the hell my card could be. I was completely panicking. Between each session, I texted Lizzy, but she hadn't found it. It was driving me up a wall because I couldn't figure out where the hell it could be. I stuck it in my pants after I paid last night. I didn't even transfer it to my wallet when I got home. I just went to bed after throwing my clothes everywhere. Lizzy had said she had searched my room, but no luck, which meant I was screwed.

On top of that, there was still another problem—my rattling loins. Yes, I said my rattling loins. Too many romance novels had ruined me. But my life was not a romance novel. If anything, it was a biography of all the dumb shit I had done in my life. Wanting to sleep with Gus Persson took up half the book. I mean, what was I even thinking? It went against everything I wanted! It went against everything I'd said! I would basically be the person he said I was if I went through with it.

But I couldn't shake the yearning I had for him.

It had to be voodoo. I swear I was fine before he opened his mouth. Before he touched me and looked at me with those sinful eyes. Before his lips moved along my cheek and my lips. I was just dandy before, but now, all I could think about was him, and I swear I could still feel his lips on mine. That was absurd!

It didn't make any sense. He wasn't worth my time!

Yet, I just wanted five minutes.

A quick, wonderful orgasm, and I'd be done.

That's all I wanted.

But first, I had to get through another lesson. Thankfully, my student's mom was cool cutting the session short, and I promised to make it up to her. I was good for it. Or at least I hoped she knew that. Once I was paid and had hugged my student, Lily, tightly, I rushed off the ice and was almost to the instructor room when I heard my name.

Or, better yet, my legal name.

"Hey! Yo, Bocephus."

My face scrunched up as I slowly looked over my shoulder, seeing the star of all my wet dreams strolling down the hall like he had no cares in the world. He looked absolutely stunning in a pair of athletic shorts and a loose tee, his hat backward with sunglasses on them. He had shaved, and he looked all clean and sexy. I bet he smelled fantastic, but that didn't matter.

Because I was *not* happy to see him.

Narrowing my eyes, I crossed my arms before leaning into the tip of my skate. "What are you doing here?"

He shrugged, such a careless motion that he somehow made sexy. "I had practice."

"Oh."

"And I'm pretty sure I have something of yours."

My brows came in. "I highly doubt that."

Reaching into his pocket, he pulled out a card, and when he held it up, I realized it was mine. I almost came out of my skates rushing to snatch it from his hands. "My card!"

I looked up, glaring. This son of a bitch stole my card! But he didn't look guilty. Instead, he was smiling as he said, "Yeah, I went to get my beer and saw it on the floor. I went outside to give it back to you, but I guess you had already left. When I went to give it to one of your friends, I wasn't sure if I could trust them, so I just kept it. Figured I'd see ya."

My face twisted in confusion. "What if you didn't see me today?"

He never stopped grinning. "Oh, I knew I would."

"How?"

Smugly, he leaned in, his eyes in line with mine as he whispered, "'Cause I wasn't going to stop until I found you."

I took in a quick breath and got lost in his gaze. I was supposed to hate this man. He was everything that had gotten me in trouble before. I knew what this kind of guy did to me. I knew the pain, the heartache, and the pure rejection, yet I had every desire to close the distance and press my lips to that lush mouth of his. I was insane, that was all there was to it. His gaze burned into mine as he took a step forward. Our bodies were so close, but then it felt like they were so far apart.

Jesus, what was wrong with me?

I swallowed hard. Breathless, I just stared at him, and then, without warning, I was hit with the memory of the dream from the night before. The vision of his lips pressing into mine fueled an erotic and molten-hot fantasy. I could feel his lips everywhere. My breasts, my stomach, my thighs, my pussy—everywhere—and looking at him right then, it was like experiencing it all over again. It made no damn sense. I almost didn't even know who I was, but just then I didn't care.

I just wanted to kiss him.
So I did.

CHAPTER NINE

GUS

Her lips were on mine without any warning whatsoever.

Not that I was complaining, but one thing was for sure, I would find anything of hers for this. Because her kiss was fucking hot and then some. Her lips were so plush and sweet. Unlike the night before, *she* was kissing *me*. She held my face in her hands as she deepened the kiss, her tongue swirling inside my mouth, and hell, I was breathless.

Fucking breathless.

No longer stunned, I reached for her, bringing her in close as our tongues moved together and our mouths nipped at each other. I thought seeing her on the ice in those tight pants as she skated had me on edge, but nothing compared to what I was feeling at that moment. Within seconds, I was harder than a goal post. I cradled her neck with one hand and gripped her lower back with the other, pulling her breasts into my chest. God, she felt so fucking good. She smelled good too, and the taste of her sweet lips hadn't left my mind since the night before.

But now, this was different. Her kisses turned urgent, her fingers digging into my cheeks as I kissed back with just as much need. I hadn't expected this to go down. I was convinced she'd make me work hard for this, but I was, thankfully, very fucking wrong.

Or so I thought.

Pulling back, gasping for breath, she looked up at me. "Oh. Oh. God."

"Oh. Oh. Yeah," I moaned before picking her up a bit, her lips crashing into mine. No doubt she was struggling with this. She didn't want to like me. I knew she didn't, but I didn't care. I wanted her.

And I wanted her fucking now.

I fully expected her to stop me when I lifted her off the ground, but to my surprise she wrapped her legs around my waist. That was all I needed. I started walking, unsure where to go, but I was going somewhere, even if it was behind the Zamboni. I didn't care. I was going to have her, and I was going to have her at that fucking moment. Pulling away, she pointed to a door.

"Here."

"Thank God," I growled against her jaw before pushing the door open and then shutting it with the weight of our bodies. Carefully, I put her to her skates as she pulled at my shirt, running her cold hands down the front of my chest. Hissing out a breath, I reached for her shirt, pulling it up and burying my face in her breasts as she cried out, arching up into me. She moved her fingers into my scalp, knocking my hat and glasses to the ground. Pulling her bra down, I took her nipple in my mouth, sucking and swirling my tongue against the hard pebble as she hissed out a breath. She leaned into me. Moving to the other breast, I took that nipple, sucking and kneading her with my hands as she arched into the door, sweet sounds falling from those naughty lips.

But I needed more.

Sliding my hand down the front of her tights, I cupped her slick and burning-hot pussy. She was pulsating, so hot between her legs. Everything inside me was wrung tight. She cried out, gasping, and then our gazes locked. I lost my breath at her beauty. Her red hair was falling out of the topknot. Her blue eyes were as dark as a thunderstorm back home. Red splotches covered her cheeks and her chin. This close I could see the freckles I had missed last night. They were everywhere, dusting her cheeks, her neck, and down the middle of her chest. I wanted to trace the spots with my tongue, get lost for hours doing only that. She was gorgeous, but when my fingers slid between her slick lips, my eyes fell shut and she wasn't the only one groaning.

To say I had been craving her was a fucking understatement. Wanting her from afar was one thing, but feeling her, touching her, and then arguing with her did nothing but make me crazy with hunger for her. I continued teasing the opening of her pussy. I was shaking so fucking hard, everything was moving, and with each pound of my heart, I swear my eyes were shaking.

"One time. Done," she muttered as I nibbled on her neck. "This won't happen again."

I was so lost I couldn't answer.

Taking her mouth with mine, I slid my fingers up her pussy to her clit, and with just one touch, she cried out against my mouth. Catching her moans, I continued to swirl the tip of my fingers along her. Wanting to give her a release. Wanting her to come all over my fingers. I wanted so desperately to hear her cry out, to savor my name falling off her lips. With each stroke, she jerked, her body moving with the motion. We should have probably taken off her skates, but neither of us had time for that.

No, and come to think of it, I needed her in my mouth.

I withdrew my hand, and she whimpered as I pulled her tights as far down as I could get them before I buried my face between the crux of her thighs. Her moans were loud and demanding as I slid my tongue up her. I swear she tasted sweeter than I could ever imagine. Opening her up, I flicked my tongue along her clit while she scraped my scalp with her fingertips. I wouldn't let up. I wanted her to come so fucking bad. I wanted to hear it, I wanted to feel it, and damn it, I wanted to taste it.

I hadn't realized I wanted her so bad, but man, did I.

It only took a few more flicks before she was coming off the door, screaming out as she jerked against my mouth. When she screamed again, I sucked her clit into my mouth, and she cried out until I saw her bite her arm. I couldn't help it... I chuckled. Sitting back on my haunches, I pulled out my wallet and grabbed a condom.

"Oh. Oh. Shit."

"Oh, I'm nowhere near done," I informed her, sliding the condom down my thick shaft before standing up and taking her legs in my arms. She cried out a bit when I pushed her knees into my chest, her skates coming dangerously close to my cock. "Whoa, let's move those."

As she held her feet to my sides, she cried out again.

"Are you okay?" I asked.

"I think I twisted my ankle."

"I made you come so hard, you twisted your ankle?"

"I hate you."

I laughed. "Are you okay?"

"It hurts," she complained, her face so red and so sexy that all I could do was grin.

"Want me to make it go away?"

She met my gaze, her eyes storm clouds as she slowly nodded. "Yes."

That was all I needed before I pushed up, my cock filling her as my hands bit into her hips. Her head fell back, her eyes falling shut as she gasped out, yet she still hadn't said my name. I wanted that so bad. More than I'd realized I did. Pressing my body into her knees, I slammed up into her, thrusting with more meaning each time, wanting my name to fall from those naughty lips of hers. But with each thrust, I noticed she grimaced a bit. I was all for having sex, but usually I liked the girl to enjoy it.

Pausing, I took in a deep breath as her gaze met mine. "Are you okay?"

"It really hurts."

"I mean, I *am* big—" I started, but she cut me off.

"No, my ankle. Like seriously."

But neither of us moved. "So I should stop?"

She glared. "Yeah."

"Really?"

"Yes, maybe I strained a tendon or something. It really

fucking hurts."

I pulled out reluctantly. When her feet hit the ground and she cried out, I got concerned. "Can you put pressure on it?"

She shook her head, tears gathering in her eyes. "Can you help me to the—" Before she could finish, though, I lifted her and took her to the bench. I sat her down and put my cock in my pants. Then I bent down to untie her skate, but before I could get the skate fully off, I could see the swelling.

Not good.

CHAPTER TEN

GUS

I hadn't been in the ER for anyone but myself, so it was kind of cool to be the one beside the gurney. I looked over at the patient, whose face was beet red with a scowl furrowing her brow, and smiled. "So this is fun."

She glared over at me. Her hair was a mess, and she had marks on her neck from where I had sucked her too hard. Her bum ankle, which I was a hundred percent sure was sprained, was up on pillows, and she looked mighty cute in her little hospital gown. But even being adorable and hot, she was pissed. Apparently she was missing school, and that was not okay. Throwing her hands up, she yelled, "How in the world is waiting two hours for someone to come get me for an X-ray fun? I told you not to come."

"You did. I came anyway." I thought after having her in my mouth she would be less hostile.

I was wrong.

"I don't even know why. What do you think? You'll get some ass for bringing me here? I don't care that you carried me and asked a billion times if I was okay! It doesn't mean anything! Also, it doesn't matter that you didn't finish, because you aren't getting any. Ever again."

Wrinkling my nose, I shook my head. "I never once mentioned anything about finishing. I'm mostly worried about your ankle."

She paused and then pressed her lips together. "That you probably broke," she snapped.

I shrugged. "I mean, I knew I was good with my mouth, but I don't take pride in breaking ankles during the act."

She looked away, and I could almost see steam coming out of her ears.

"I would never intentionally hurt you."

"I don't care."

"Okay," I said simply, leaning back in my chair. Her lips were in a little pout and her eyes full of fire as she looked down at her ankle, almost cursing it. "So you're missing school?"

She exhaled hard, the frustration all over her face. "Yes."

"What are you going to school for?"

She looked over at me, and if looks could kill... "Why does it matter?"

"Just making conversation. We've been sitting for a while in silence or with you yelling at someone, so I thought we'd kill some time."

She exhaled hard, looking away as she crossed her arms. "Physical therapy."

I nodded. "Cool. Do you like it?"

She shrugged. "It's fine."

"But?"

She was annoyed, I could see that. But I wanted to know.

"It's not what I wanted. I wanted to be a doctor."

I nodded, impressed. "Why didn't you do that instead?"

"I lost my scholarship," she said softly. "There was no way I could go into that kind of debt, and my parents couldn't afford it. Not everyone has the silver spoon from Mommy and Daddy."

Her eyes cut to me, and I shrugged. "Isn't my fault my parents have money."

"And you have no problems reaping the benefits either."

I looked away. "Who says I do?" When I looked over at her, our gazes locked. "I haven't used a lick of my parents' money since I signed my contract with the Tornadoes. Yeah, that's only been a little over six months, but I haven't."

She looked away, inhaling hard before letting it out slowly through her nose. I watched as she uncrossed her arms and twisted her fingers together. She seemed uncomfortable, and I sorta liked that look on her. Swallowing hard, she looked back at me, but just as her lips began to move, the curtain opened.

"Hey! I'm Angie! Here to take you for your X-ray!"

I looked away from her as Bo nodded. "Great."

"Okay, can you walk?"

Bo shook her head. "Not really."

"Oh," Angie said.

I reached to help Bo stand, but before I could touch her, she held a hand up. "What are you doing?"

"I'm going to pick you up and put you in the wheelchair Angie forgot."

Angie then disappeared.

Bo looked up at me. "Why?" she asked.

"Because I don't want you to hurt yourself even more

trying to get in the chair, and Angie can't lift you."

Without her permission, I lifted her with ease. For a thick chick, she was light to me, and I liked that. Instantly, my mind traveled back to the rink, to when I carried her in that room and took what I wanted.

Well, that is until she snapped her ankle.

Which sucked.

She wrapped her hands around my neck, and I smiled at her.

"This means nothing," she said. Her words were sharp, but there was something in her tone that let me know she remembered what we'd just shared at the rink.

"Of course not," I answered as I slowly put her down in the chair that Angie brought.

"Your boyfriend—"

"He is not my boyfriend," Bo corrected.

"Friend—"

"Nope. Acquaintance," she said.

I grinned. "Hey, at least I'm something."

She did not like that, and poor Angie looked confused as she rolled Bo away. She sure was cute, which was probably why I took her abuse. Though, once I got her to let go of all her hostility, I thought we'd get along really well. I sat down in my seat with a smile as I pulled my phone out, scrolling through Facebook. When a message came through from Max, my brow rose.

Max: *Dude, where are you?*

Looking at the time, I cursed.

Gus: *Shit. Sorry, dude. I'm not going to make it.*

Max: *But I can't watch Survivor without you!*

Gus: *Yeah, don't you dare. I'll be pissed, but I'm still up at the hospital with Bo.*

Max: *Who the hell is Bo?*

Gus: *Hot redhead.*

Max: *That blew you off?*

Gus: *That's her. We're cool now.*

Max: *lol So you think. She'll probably kill you by the end of the night.*

Looking at Maxy's words over and over again, I couldn't shake that he was right. What was I doing? This girl was obviously not into me—well, she was into me enough to have a hot quickie, but once she came out of that orgasm cloud, the unfriendliness was back. Why was I even still here? She didn't need me. She'd made that plenty clear, yet, I didn't want to leave. I wanted to make sure she was okay. I wanted to drive her home.

I really wanted her to like me.

Shit.

I tucked my phone into my pocket and closed my eyes as I

waited. Thankfully, I didn't have to wait long until the curtain opened and Bo was being brought back in.

I stood. "Were you a good girl?"

Bo flicked me off as I reached for her.

Angie patted my bicep. "I could use you around here." Her tone was very suggestive, and when I looked up, meeting her gaze, it was obvious the hot nurse wanted a piece of me.

But I just laughed her off while I helped Bo get into bed and rest her foot on a pillow. "I get that a lot."

Angie lingered a little longer than she should have before she left, and then I sat down. "You okay?"

Bo looked over at me. "You know she was hitting on you?"

I nodded. "I do."

With a deadpan look, she pointed to the curtain. "So shouldn't you go try to sleep with her or something?"

I shook my head, crossing my legs as I held her gaze. "I'm good where I am."

Her eyes darkened, and I swear I saw a little joy flicker in those eyes. "I told you, this is nothing."

"I never said it was."

With exasperation all over her face, she leaned back against the pillows with a huff. Silence stretched as she pouted, and I knew it was from the pain. She couldn't have that much animosity toward me after I made her come. That would be rude, and she wasn't rude. She was just bitter. Someone really must have done a number on her.

And I wanted to know who.

Clearing my throat, I asked, "So, who did you dirty?"

Her face twisted in confusion and annoyance before she

faced me. "What?"

"What guy did you dirty? Someone did something, because you hate me for shit I haven't even done."

"Yet."

I rolled my eyes. "I can read you like a book, Bocephus, and let me tell you, I wanted you because that ass of yours is juicy and your hair sets my soul on fire. I think you're hot, but I also like that you try to hate me but can't. It's adorable."

Her eyes narrowed, but she paused, which meant I was right. "I hate you just fine."

"Nope, I know I'm right."

She rolled her eyes. "You're delusional."

I laughed, kicking my legs up on her bed, careful not to bump her bum ankle. "It's okay to admit it."

"Never."

Her face was all squished up, but I knew the truth. "So we're friends now, right?"

She laughed. "Not even close."

"Sure we are. We are learning about each other."

"No, you're running your mouth."

I scoffed, looking down at my hands. I liked her. I liked her fieriness, and I especially like that she wasn't fawning over me. She might do it in her head, but she wouldn't allow me to ever know that. That turned me on.

A lot.

"So when can I take you to dinner?"

CHAPTER ELEVEN

BO

What in the absolute hell?

"Are you insane? Have you not heard one word I've said this whole time?"

"No, we're vibing."

I could only stare at him, dumbfounded. "Vibing?"

"Yes, when you're not fighting it, we get along."

Still dumbfounded, I asked, "Fighting it?"

"The passion," he said simply, moving his hands between us. "It's so thick, we could cut it with a knife."

"There is no passion."

He gave me a look, one that curled his lips while his eyes zoned in on me, dark as night. "Girl, there is so much passion we both almost caught on fire back at the rink. I don't know why you feel you need to say no, but you don't. You can say yes. I know you want me."

His ego was so damn big, I was honestly shocked there was room for the rest of the world. Holding up my hand, I said, "Okay, pause. One, brief lapse of judgment was what happened at the rink. I was horny, I was upset about losing my card, and you were in the right place at the right time. Second—"

Before I could finish, though, he was out of his seat, leaning so close his nose almost touched mine. "Is that what you keep telling yourself, over and over again, with the hopes it pushes down the pure raw passion that is swirling in your gut for me?"

Breathless, I couldn't move, my gaze held hostage by his.

"'Cause I get it. You don't want to be tied down to someone like me—hell, you don't even have to admit you like me. I'm not asking for forever, pumpkin. I'm asking for right now."

What in the world was he doing to me? It was like I was in a trance as he slid his finger along my jaw.

"I just want to finish what we started back at the rink and then some. I want to lick you from the tip of that nose to the center of your pussy. I want to rake my teeth along your clit and hear you scream my name. I want to fuck you until your knees are weak and you can't breathe."

Pushing against his chest with my hands, I took in a deep, composing breath. "Not gonna happen. I don't like you."

He scoffed, but I could see the pang of my rejection swirling in his eyes. "You keep saying that, but your body is saying something completely different."

Stupid body. "My body is saying nothing."

He scoffed again. "Actually," he whispered, and then he moved in close once more. "It's saying fuck me. Fuck me hard, Gus. So hard."

I pushed him away again and rolled my eyes. "How many times do I gotta say no until it clicks?"

He crossed his arms across his chest. "It won't. I get what I want."

"Well, not today, buddy, or tomorrow. Or the next day," I added for good measure. "I don't have time for your shenanigans."

He chuckled at that. "And what shenanigans would that entail?"

Why did I say that? Rolling my eyes, I leaned back in the bed and shrugged. "Who knows? You'd probably fall in love with me. I mean, I *am* amazing."

His lips curved. "Now who's the cocky one?"

I couldn't help it. I grinned. He wasn't as bad as I thought, or maybe I was being wooed by the fact that he hadn't left my side since I got hurt. No one had ever done that for me. It was nice. Plus, he was funny, but none of that mattered. I couldn't do it. "Gus, really, I'm just not down for that. I have too much going on."

He didn't miss a beat. "I said one night. Dinner, movie, sex, sex, and more sex."

It sounded nice. And man, I hadn't been out with a guy in forever. But I couldn't risk it. Not with him. Gus was dangerous. And the problem was, he knew it. "No. I'm good."

He shook his head. "You'll give in."

"No, I won't."

"Yeah, you will," he answered so damn confidently I couldn't help but admire it. He was sure of himself. Proud too. If only he wasn't so obnoxiously cocky about it, I may have considered it.

Rolling my eyes, I looked toward the ground, refusing to give him an answer. We had been waiting forever, and I was getting antsy. I was pissed I was missing classes, though Lizzy said she'd bring me the notes.

I really hated how attracted I was to him. He was just so handsome and rugged, and I swore I would never forget the feel of that mouth between my legs. Or the tips of his fingers between my thighs. It was over before it started, and man, I wanted round two and maybe three, but in just those three minutes with him, I was already starting to get lost.

Just like I did with Jesse, and that was a clusterfuck I did not want to relive. Yet, I still found it really sweet that Gus was waiting with me. That he had carried me there. That he cared. It showed another side that wasn't the cocky asshole I pegged him to be. Gus looked over at me and smiled. Sweet and oh so sexy.

"You can leave," I told him. "I can have a friend come get me."

He shook his head. "I'm good," he answered with ease, and he was about to say more, but the curtain opened and in came a doctor.

"Bo St. James?"

I held up my hand but before either of us could say anything, Gus was laughing. "Bocephus Jane St. James?" He laughed some more. "Are you sure your parents loved you?"

I glared, looking at him through my lashes. "Shut up." The nice doctor was confused as she looked back to me. "Yes, that's me."

"Okay, Ms. St. James, it looks like you have one hell of a sprain. I want you to stay completely off it for a week. No weight. Only use the crutches."

Oh, fuck me.

Panic filled my chest as she went on. "After a week, I want you to go to your PCP and go from there. Here are some pain meds, and here is the order for your crutches. I'm sure your boyfriend can get them for you before you leave."

Annoyed, I sneered, "He isn't my boyfriend."

The doctor looked back, her eyes full of appreciation. "Well, my advice is, change that," she said with a wink. Gus was grinning ear to ear. "The nurse will come in here to wrap you up and get you going. It was nice meeting you. Sorry for the wait."

"Thank you," I said.

She was gone then, leaving me in the room with Gus, who was still grinning so damn big, I was blinded by his teeth.

"Stop smiling. It's intolerable."

"'Cause you want me?"

I shook my head, looking down as I covered my face so I wouldn't be distracted by him. I wasn't sure what I was going to do.

"I am so screwed."

"What do you mean?"

I hadn't realized I had said that out loud.

I couldn't work without both feet. School would be fine, but I had to work. Well, I might be able to exchange the ice barrels at the games, but my private lessons and my ice skating classes? Fuck, I was screwed. They'd replace me without even a second thought! "Shit."

"What?"

Shaking my head, I blew out a breath. "I can't work. I'm going to lose my classes and clients at the rink."

"Ice skating, you say?"

I looked over at him. "Yeah."

When that sly grin came back and his eyes burned into mine, I was pretty sure I was in trouble. "Well, Ms. Bocephus Jane St. James, or as I like to call you, BJSJ, I am a great ice skater. I did it my whole childhood, I can teach your classes with you."

I laughed at the absurdity of it. "You don't want to waste your time on me and my kids. I can't pay you. I really do need the money."

"That's fine. I don't need your money. I just want to help," he said simply.

"Why?"

"Because it's kinda my fault you got that busted ankle." When he waggled his brows at me, I rolled my eyes.

"I don't know. Do you even know anything about figure skating?"

He flashed me a grin. "Actually, my mom is a coach back home. That's how I got into hockey. I started in figure skating, but then I didn't like how tight the pants were, so she put me in hockey."

This was all very surprising. I thought maybe he came from a long line of hockey players. "Oh," I said, and then I made a face. "Your mom worked?"

He shrugged. "Yeah, we work for what we want. She wanted more purses and shoes, so she worked."

That made me smile. "Oh." Well that was interesting.

He gave me an exaggerated wink. "Told ya you don't know me."

And if I was honest with myself, I wanted to know more. Did I have him all wrong? No, I didn't. He was too flashy and too obnoxious to not come from loads of money.

With a flash of a grin, he said, "I'll do a great job."

I didn't doubt that. He was obviously a great skater, but how could I take help from the one guy I was supposed to stay away from? I didn't know anyone else who could fill in. The girls I worked with all had their own clients, and I couldn't risk my students getting taken from me. I needed the income, and I loved the little buggers. Plus, this could work to my advantage. There would be no goofing off if some hot guy was there to teach them. I knew the girls would eat him up. *Shit*. Was I saying yes?

Shit.

Ugh.

"There is a catch, though."

I furrowed my brow. "I should have known."

He chuckled. "It won't be that awful."

"Whatever, Bus. What's the catch?"

His grin grew, his pearly whites flashing as he went on. "Well, Bocephus, I do this, and you go on a date with me."

I glared. Not because he used my real name but because he was insane if he thought that would work. "What? Seriously?"

"Yes. At the end of the week, we go out."

"I don't want to go out with you."

"Then you don't want my help, and let's be honest, no one else can help you the way I can. You know that's true."

I stared at him as I racked my brain for anyone else who could do it. Blinking, I went through everyone I could trust.

That list was very short. Actually, there was only Lizzy, and she didn't figure skate; she only ice skated. I realized in that moment I had no one, and it was a very scary feeling. Especially since I was about to depend on the one person I swore to hate.

I was about to say something I never thought I would say. Something I promised myself I wouldn't say.

Yes.

CHAPTER TWELVE

GUS

I was pretty sure by the look on Bo's face that she'd rather take a puck to the mouth than see me walking toward her. I didn't care though. She looked good—great, even, with her leggings and large sweatshirt that reached almost to the bottom of her thighs. Her hair was in a long braid down her shoulder, and she was makeup free, looking as if she had just rolled out of bed. But those eyes were in slits, and she did not look happy.

"I sort of thought you wouldn't show up," she called to me, and then her face twisted in confusion. "What's that? I thought you said you knew how to skate!"

I placed the balance checker in front of her. "It's for you. I figured you can come out on the ice with us and just follow carefully."

Her face relaxed, but she held back the smile. "Oh. I didn't think of that."

"Yeah, my mom tore her ACL when I was like nine, and she had to do it this way."

"Oh," she said. I was starting to love the way she said that word. Her lips formed a perfect circle for my cock to fit right into. Was I wrong for thinking that?

I didn't think so either.

Tearing my gaze from her mouth, I looked down at her ankle. "How you feeling?"

I had taken her home the night before. She lived about six blocks from me, in a sublet that she and a friend were sharing. It was a nice location, but she wouldn't let me take her upstairs. Her friend had come down to help, which upset me. I wanted to help her. I wanted to be there for her, and it was annoying that she wouldn't let me. I wasn't sure what her deal was, but I was going to find out.

When I looked up, she shrugged, grimacing a bit. "It's achy, but I'll be fine."

"Did you keep it elevated?"

She shot me a deadpan look. "I know how to take care of myself."

"Not saying you don't. I just want to make sure."

She swallowed hard and nodded. "I did."

"Good." I wished I'd been there helping her. I'd spent all night worrying and wishing I had gotten her number so I could check on her. "Hey, you should give me your number."

Her brows pulled together as her lips pursed. "For what?"

This time it was me with the deadpan look. "In case I'm stuck in traffic or something and I'll be late."

"So you won't text me dick pics?"

I laughed, surprised. "Not today, but maybe next week," I said with a wink, and she rolled her eyes before handing me her phone.

"Do as you please."

"Oh man, wrong thing to say to someone like me," I teased, but she wasn't listening. She was leaning on the balance checker.

"Cute kid," I said, holding the phone up. "Your brother, right?"

Something moved in her eyes, but it was gone quickly, and her eyes narrowed as she reached for her phone.

I held it up out of her reach. "I'm not done. What's his name?"

She seemed uncomfortable as she said it. "Davis."

"Oh? They didn't name him Hank? Or Bocephus Jr.?"

She laughed, and it was a real laugh. From her stomach as her eyes closed a bit, but then she stopped abruptly. "I must be high to think that was funny," she muttered, and now I was laughing as I typed in my number. "No, actually, I wouldn't let them."

I nodded. "Well, he's gonna love you extra hard when he's older."

"Probably not," she muttered, but before I could ask what she meant, she looked up at me, her bright-blue eyes burning into mine. "How are your jumps?"

I shrugged. "Good. I mean, I haven't practiced them in a while, but I'm sure I still got it."

She nodded, biting her lip. "We're working on her Salchow jump. She's almost got it."

I scoffed, waving her off. "Oh, I have that easy. Let me get my skates on. When's she gonna be here, and what's her name?"

"Tenisha, and she'll be here in about ten. I asked for you to be early so we can go over a few things."

My brows rose. "What things? Need my credentials? Wanna call my mom?"

She waved me off. "No, I need you to know that I take my job seriously. There will be no playing around."

I nodded. "Check."

"And don't flirt with me."

"In front of the kids, right?"

"At all when we're on the ice."

I made a face. "That's hard, though. You're so hot."

She shook her head. "For real. I take this completely seriously, and I need you to realize that. I depend on this money."

There was desperation in her voice, and I didn't understand it. My work ethic was sound. I didn't get why she would assume it wouldn't be here. "Fine, I'll be completely professional. I won't let you down."

She swallowed hard and then nodded. "Thank you." She looked past me and then smiled. "There she is. Let's do this."

I held up my fist. "Yeah, let's kick ass."

Her eyes widened a bit, but she pressed her fist to mine and smiled. "Yeah. Don't embarrass me, please."

Before I could say anything, she was wobbling away, and I couldn't help but grin.

Because I was excited to prove her wrong.

♦ ♦ ♦ ♦

Bo was sucking on her lips as she tapped her good sneaker into the rubber floor. Her lips were pursed, and her hair was a little messy from trying to demonstrate. When she couldn't do it, she ran her fingers through her hair angrily. Her face was red, her nose especially, as she moved her hands through the air. I wasn't sure what she was doing, so I just sat there, waiting for her to speak to me.

We had finished all her privates. All the girls were great, and I enjoyed working with them. They were adorable, but I especially loved watching Bo with them. She was so motherly and gushed on them. She was nothing like my mom, who did a whole lot of yelling and direction. Bo was nicer, which surprised me, given how bitchy she was most of the time.

She especially had a soft spot for the little skaters. I guess I did too. We went over time with Amelia because she was trying so hard to get her leap and we wanted her to get it. It was fun—lots of fun—and I didn't regret coming to help instead of going out with the guys for a beer. I wanted to be here.

With Bo.

"So that was cool. Will we have the same girls all week, or do they come weekly?"

She looked down at me. I was sitting on the bench, untying my skates. Clearing her throat, she tucked her hands into the sleeve holes of her shirt. "We'll have two of them on Thursday, but other than that, they all come next week."

"Cool. Do we get Tenisha again? She's going to get that jump; I'll make sure of it."

She smiled. "Yeah, she comes on Thursday."

"Awesome." I flashed her a grin before looking down to take my skate off. "So was I on my best behavior?"

When I looked up, she was struggling again. It was sort

of funny, but she nodded, a smile curling her lips. "You did fantastic. I thought I was going to have to do a lot more. You are actually really great."

"Yeah, I'm basically great at everything."

When she rolled her eyes, I couldn't help but laugh.

"Anyway, I appreciate you helping me. Thank you."

"Anytime. Honestly. I had a blast," I said as I slid my feet into my sandals. Standing up, letting my skates hang from my fingers, I smiled down at her. "Wanna go get a drink?"

She shook her head almost immediately, like she knew what I was going to say. "I can't drink on my pain meds."

"We can get food and a bottle of water."

She looked away, shaking her head. "I can't. I've got homework and makeup shit since I missed last night."

I nodded. "That's right."

"Yeah, so—"

"I'll walk you out."

She didn't want me to, I could tell, but I wanted to. Dropping to her speed since she was hobbling on crutches, I walked beside her in silence until I asked, "So, you said that you depend on the money. Do you not make much as an ice girl?"

She laughed out loud, looking up at me like I was kidding. "Oh, you're serious?" She laughed a little more, and I realized she must have made shit. "I make forty dollars a game."

I made a face. "That's totally not worth it. I mean, just with all the shit the players put you guys through."

She nodded. "The girls like it."

"You don't."

"No one really messes with me, and all you do is stare."

That made me unbelievably happy. I didn't want to beat up anyone on my team. I liked the guys. "Well, when I see a gorgeous girl, I gotta check her out."

She blushed a bit as she looked down, watching where she was going.

"So, you depend on this, then?"

She nodded. "I make a lot here, I've built a great clientele, and everyone loves me."

"You're great with them."

"Thank you."

"So you were a figure skater?"

"I was, all growing up, but I wasn't good enough to do anything with it. I'm really smart though, so I got a full scholarship without skating."

I smiled. "That's awesome." I paused, hoping that she would ask me something, but she didn't. So I asked, "So you're not paying for school?"

She shook her head. "No, I pay for most of it. I only got a partial scholarship to MPT."

"I thought you said you got a full scholarship?"

"Yeah. That was for an Ivy League school."

"But you didn't go?"

"Nope, I lost that."

"Why?"

She shrugged. "Mistakes."

"Like?"

"Stuff," she said, waving her hand at me. "I'm not telling you."

"Yet."

"Or ever. We aren't friends."

I laughed at that. "Of course we are. We're practically besties."

"If your friends treat you the way I do, then I would suggest you get some new friends."

I smiled. "Nah, they're cool, but you're my favorite."

"You don't even know me."

"Because you won't let me, but just think, we have a date on Saturday, and I'll learn all kinds of things. Like how many freckles are on that sweet pussy of yours."

Reaching out, she smacked my chest. "There could be kids out here."

I shrugged innocently. "Hey, we're not on the ice."

She rolled her eyes, looking out in the parking lot. "Whatever."

Holding the door for her, I asked, "Can you drive?"

She nodded. "Yeah, I'm fine. Thanks." She wobbled to her car. "Bye, Gus the Bus."

I laughed. "See ya, BJSJ."

I was answered by her laughter, and I couldn't think of a better way for our night to end.

Problem was, I wanted more.

A lot more.

CHAPTER THIRTEEN

BO

Gus moved with ease.

It was almost like he floated on the ice. The way he held his stick, it was like it was part of him. He moved around people like they weren't even there. His puck handling was downright sick, and when he shot from the point, I was convinced he wouldn't make it, but he did—with no effort at all. It seemed like he knew the puck would go in before he even let his stick slam into it. It was insane, but I would be lying if I said I didn't love watching him play. I enjoyed it immensely. Not that I would ever admit that to him.

He'd let it go to his head, and since Gus Persson's head was big enough for an army, I wouldn't contribute to that. I'd watch him, though.

Leaning on my shovel, I kept my chin on the handle and leaned my hips into the bar, putting more of my weight on my good leg. I watched as he skated the rink like he owned it. In a way, he did. The puck always found its way to his stick. His teammates loved him. The crowd loved him. Shit, everyone loved him. Well, everyone except me. I had to stay smart when it came to Gus.

I had to keep him at arm's length, though it was becoming very hard. I really appreciated everything he was helping me with. He was amazing with kids, and he had the patience of a saint. But he wasn't the guy for me, and that was that. Yeah, I had agreed to go out with him, but I had decided that it would be a one-time deal. After that, we'd go our separate ways, no hard feelings, no nothing.

Or at least that's what I kept telling myself.

I held my breath as Gus stormed toward the goal, right in front of where I was standing. He had such determination on his face. His eyes narrowed with the goal in sight as he moved the puck with a quickness that I was convinced only hockey players possessed. When a defenseman tried to cut him off, he passed it up to no one, but then he was there, grabbing the puck and rushing the goal once more. He deked right and then right once more, pulling the goalie completely out, but instead of shooting then, even with an open goal, he spun around and backhanded it in.

Like a fucking boss.

An obnoxious boss, but a boss, nonetheless.

I cried out, surprising myself. I threw my arms in the air, and the shovel toppled to the ground. What the hell was I doing? I was immediately embarrassed at my reaction and tried to reach down for my shovel. But Lizzy was there, handing it to me with a look on her face.

"Hmmmmm."

I rolled my eyes. "Hmm what?"

"Oh nothing," she said, a little grin pulling at her lips. "Just hmm."

The whistle blew for an ice cleaning, and I stuck my tongue out at her. "There is no reason for hmm."

She just smiled. "Oh, of course not." Her eyes were all-knowing as she rushed out onto the ice. I hobbled to the door and handed my shovel to another girl as I held the trash can for her to fill. Emily wasn't much of a talker. I was pretty sure she hadn't said more than two words to me, but she was quick as hell on the ice. She scooped the ice and dumped it in, but for some reason, I wasn't paying attention.

I was watching Gus.

Like a dumbass.

Squirting water into his mouth, he licked his lips as some of it dripped down his chin onto his jersey. A grin was on his lips, his eyes bright as he leaned into the boards, talking to his teammates. When he squirted more water in his mouth, I held on to the trash can, my whole body going hot. Pulling his jersey out, he squirted the water down his chest, his neck, and then all over his face.

He was *hot*.

And I don't mean the temperature.

It was utterly sinful the way the water dripped down his sharp angles and caught in the stubble on his jaw. My pussy clenched at the sight, and I wanted to lick every single drop off his face, his neck...hell, his body. I didn't care. I was suddenly so damn parched that I couldn't think of anything but that water in my mouth.

Hell, all of Gus in my mouth.

Jesus, what the hell is wrong with me?

But before I could even try to figure that out, he turned, his gaze meeting mine as he wiped his chin with his hand in such a simple movement but, I swore, an erotic one. His eyes were dark and when his tongue came out, wetting his lips even more, my knuckles gripping the trash can went white within seconds. When his lips started to curve, his teeth slowly showing as he held my gaze, I wanted so bad to look away, to flick him off just to show I didn't care, but I couldn't move.

Not even when Emily missed the whole trash can and covered me with the excess ice.

"Oh, shit, Bo. I'm so sorry."

Still I couldn't answer. I just shrugged, moving my hands down the front of my little uniform. I should have been worried. Really worried.

Because not even the ice was able to cool me down at that moment.

And that was bad.

Very fucking bad.

◆ ◆ ◆ ◆

Lying back in my bed, my ankle perched up on a pillow, I worked on some homework that I had left until the last minute. It wasn't like me to wait so long to finish, but I had been distracted. Between my ankle and hoping that Gus didn't embarrass me at work, I had reasons to be distracted, but that just validated my issues with Gus even more. He was nothing but trouble. I knew this, yet my thoughts kept swirling back to him.

Shit, I was two seconds from drawing little hearts on my homework.

Groaning, I shook my head as I went back to work, pushing aside any and every thought of Gus. I was doing great, until my door opened and Lizzy popped her head in. "Hey."

I looked up, a smile on my face. "Hey."

She came in, falling down on the bed, careful of my foot as she leaned on her hands. "So, I think I'm going to go out with Roger."

My face twisted in confusion. "Roger as in Roger McMillian, our professor?"

She shrugged, a grin curving her lips in an innocent but oh-so-wrong way. "Yeah, he's not like a *professor* professor. Come on."

"He's still our professor," I stressed. "I'm pretty sure that is against the rules."

She smiled. "It's frowned upon, but he said he'll do it if I want to. And I do."

I rolled my eyes. "He's like forty."

"He's only thirty-one."

"That's ten years older than you!"

"So? He's hot."

He was, but still. "Lizzy, you can find someone your age."

"Age is just a number," she said, waving me off. "Plus, I really want to get laid and by a man."

My face scrunched up. "Are you having sex with females and I didn't know it?"

She laughed, rolling onto her back. "No, I mean, I want a man who is going to love every single inch of me. Not a selfish man, where I'm sucking his dick for an hour and getting a finger shoved up my puss as his foreplay. I want someone to take his time with me."

And just like that, my thoughts flew back to Gus. Squirming in the bed, I nodded. "Yeah, I guess..."

"Come on! You know what I mean, like a guy who will stay between my legs for hours with his mouth. Someone who is worried about my orgasm. Someone who cares about pleasing me. All these guys just want to come and don't care about me, ya know?"

Swallowing hard, I tried to calm my body, but it was useless. Between my dream and having Gus between my legs in real life and then seeing him with water dripping down that mouth of his and thinking that could have been the remnants of my orgasm, there was no way I could think of anything but. Gus was just like Lizzy was describing, not that she knew that. I did not tell her. Anything. Involving Gus...

Not that it mattered. It was my business. I answered, "Yeah."

"Good, I'm glad you agree."

Since I didn't want to argue with her, and hell, it wasn't my life, I nodded. "You do you, Liz."

She smiled happily as she rolled on her stomach, eyeing me. "So things with Gus going well?"

I made a face, trying to hide my panic. "Things? There is nothing."

"Bo, he's helping you at the rink. And I saw the way you looked at him tonight."

I waved her off. "Please, that was nothing. He's the reason my ankle is busted."

She pulled her brows together and pursed her lips as she

pointed to me. "I thought you said you tripped and twisted it."

I nodded. I'd forgotten that was what I told her. "I tripped over him! He's got big ole feet."

She scoffed. "You're lying to me, you asshole."

I laughed. Nervously. "I would never."

"Whatever. I know something is going on."

"Nothing is going on," I said once more, waving her off, and then I pointed to the door. "Go on. I've got work to do."

She rolled her eyes, scooting off the bed. "I know something is, but fine. I'll let you lie and try to keep him all to yourself."

As she got off the bed, I gave her a look. "Nothing is going on."

She just laughed. "Fine, but remember, Bo St. James, be careful. Gus isn't the kind of guy to settle down."

I rolled my eyes. "There is nothing to be careful about. For one, I'm not settling down, and for two, nothing is going on."

"That's what they all say when it comes to Gus the Bus," she sang as she went out the door, shutting it behind her before I could say anything else. Not sure what I would have said, but either way, it wasn't going to happen. I might have thought he was hot as sin and cool when he wasn't being a pigheaded, obnoxious fuck boy, but that was only ten percent of the time. The other ninety percent, I hated him.

And that was that.

When my phone sounded, I reached for it, and just like that, my granny was in my head, speaking her famous phrase. *Speak of the devil, and he shall appear.*

Gus: *Hey, how's the ankle?*

I almost didn't text him back. We'd exchanged numbers so that if anything came up this week, he could get ahold of me or the other way around. This was not allowed.

Bo: *Are you going to be late tomorrow?*

Gus: *No. I was just checking in.*

Bo: *You don't need to check in unless you aren't coming.*

Gus: *Fuck, BJSJ, calm down. I'm just saying hey and checking in on your ankle. I was worried about you.*

That stupid nickname he had for me was going to get on my last nerve. Especially since it made me grin like a stupid schoolgirl. And then I got another text from him.

Gus: *If you don't tell me, I'll call.*

Damn it. Rolling my eyes, I threw my pencil on the bed and typed back violently.

Bo: *My ankle is fine.*

Gus: *Good. Keeping it elevated?*

Bo: *Yes.*

Gus: *Great. Is the swelling going down?*

Bo: *Some.*

Gus: *Great, you'll be back to normal in no time. It killed me seeing you by the doors today.*

My face scrunched up. Why did he care?

Bo: *Why?*

Gus: *You looked bored. Plus, I couldn't check out your ass and tits from where I was. It was depressing.*

I didn't respond, caught for a moment in the thought of him checking me out while I'd been so unbelievably hot for him.

Gus: *Are you trying to ignore me?*

Bo: *I have nothing to say, I'm trying to finish my homework.*

Gus: *I bet you'd have a lot to say if I sent you a dick pic.*

Bo: *Don't you dare.*

Gus: *lol What… Will it turn you on?*

Bo: *I'm going to get back to my schoolwork.*

Gus: *Okay, I won't send it.*

Good. That was good. I reached for my pencil as my phone went off once more.

Gus: *Unless you want me to.*

Bo: *I don't.*

Gus: *Maybe after Saturday.*

Bo: *You're still holding me to that?*

Gus: *Fuck yeah, I am. I'm going to wine, dine, and fuck you so damn hard, you won't know what's happening.*

Instantly my pussy clenched and I gasped, gripping the pencil in one hand and the phone in the other. Holy shit. Trying to keep some sense of space between us, I typed back quickly.

Bo: *I highly doubt that.*

Gus: *You just wait.*

Bo: *I mean, I'm not going to count down the days or anything.*

Gus: *I am. The minutes, actually.*

Unsure what to say, I threw my phone down and repeated

Lizzy's words, over and over again.

Be careful, be careful...be...careful...

My phone sounded once more, and when I opened my eyes, they widened when I read what he had to say.

Gus: *If I almost broke your ankle before, no telling what I'm going to rip apart when I get you in my bed. So be ready, BJSJ, because I am.*

Swallowing hard, I reached over, shutting my phone off. Because if I didn't, Gus was going to make me swoon. And that just couldn't happen.

CHAPTER FOURTEEN

GUS

"So you're helping a girl because you broke her ankle?"

I knew my mom was covering up her laughter. I had called her for some tips on my jumps since I was determined to get these girls their jumps before I stopped helping. Since I wasn't sure how much longer that would be, I figured today was the day.

"Do I even want to know how you did that?"

My grin was wide as I shrugged. "Well, you know, Mom."

"I know I raised you better than to hurt some poor girl."

I scoffed at that. "I can promise you, this girl is nowhere near a poor girl. She's like you. An asshole."

She laughed hard at that. "Seems like my kind of girl."

"You'd love her."

She scoffed, and at the familiar sound, I missed her so damn bad. She'd had me early, so she wasn't like other moms. She was sixteen when she had me, so in some sense, I looked to her as a friend. Though, she did beat my ass a lot. Especially when my dad came back into her life. "Not that I'll ever meet her."

I wasn't sure how to answer that. "Eh."

"Just like your father—screw and leave them."

"Hey, you married him."

She laughed. "Ah, he's rich."

I laughed too, knowing that wasn't the reason at all. She loved my father and was devastated when he left her way back when. "So that's why I was asking about the jumps. She's a coach, and since I almost broke her ankle, I offered to help."

"Or you offered because you like her more than just a wham, bam, thank you, ma'am."

"Mom, no one talks like that anymore."

"Whatever! I just heard Martha say it at the country club!"

"You did not!"

She snickered. "Okay, maybe she was making fun of me because I said it, but she said it."

"Stop embarrassing Dad and yourself there."

She chuckled, and I heard my dad in the background laughing. "Those old farts love us."

"'Cause of Dad," I reminded her.

My dad agreed. "I tell her that, but she doesn't listen."

"I know," I said, moving around the rink, the crunch of the ice under my skates feeding my soul.

"Great game last night," Dad said.

"Thanks. I only got a goal."

"Son, you've scored in every game you've played."

I shrugged, even though he couldn't see me. "Even still, I haven't been called up yet."

"Which I feel is bullshit," Mom said.

I smiled. "Agreed."

"Agreed too," Dad said with a chuckle. "But don't worry,

they will. I think you're the best."

"You have to say that... You abandoned me for seven years, and now you're trying to win back my love."

"Shit, I won that back a long time ago."

"You did, but I'm still bitter."

That had both my parents laughing, and all I could do was grin as I skated around. I didn't realize I was watching the door until it opened and Bo was hobbling through it. "Hey, I gotta go. I'll call you guys tonight?"

"Of course, baby. I love you."

"I love you more than she does."

I scoffed. "God, Dad, I get it. You're still a bit insecure. I love you. I do."

Hanging up on their laughter, I tucked my phone into my pocket, skating to where Bo was entering the players' box. "Hey."

She looked over at me, but she didn't smile. Her hair was down in curls, and she had a little bit of makeup on today. It accented her face perfectly. Her eyes were bright, though it may have been the bright-blue sweatshirt she was wearing that was doing that. Her leggings were, thankfully, tight and hugging that ass in the way I loved. When I saw that she had one regular boot on while her other was in the boot the doctor had given her, I just smiled. She was so fucking adorable.

The best part, though, was that her lips were plump and a red color that had me harder than a stack of pucks.

"God, you're hot."

Her cheeks filled with color as she rolled her eyes. "I told you to behave while you're here."

"Hey, I see no kids."

"But my boss could come through at any moment."

I smiled. "I'll tell her the same."

She giggled. "It's a him."

I laughed. "I am comfortable with who I am as a man to be able to tell another man he is hot."

"He's like sixty."

"Hey, the older the better."

She snickered as she placed her bag down. "You're insane."

"Some would agree." Placing my hands on the boards, I swung my legs in and out of the doorway. "Hot date?"

Giving me a look, she shook her head. "No."

"So why do you look so sexy?"

"I don't," she said. She moved her hands through her hair, pulling it up. "I had my internship today."

"Oh, cool. Over at the compound?"

She nodded.

"So if I feign an injury, I get to have you rub me down?"

She paused from pulling her hair up. "Why do I have a feeling you'll try that?"

"Because I would," I laughed.

"Please don't." She smiled.

"Why? Couldn't handle it? Rubbing my naked body and having to stay professional?"

Rolling her eyes, she pushed my chest, but before she could pull her hand back, I snatched it in mine, pulling her close to me. She didn't have much control and went off balance, right into my arms. While I wished she had grinned up at me, she was glaring. "What are you doing?"

I shrugged. "Anything you want."

She rolled her eyes, righting herself the best she could as she looked over at me. "Which is nothing."

I scoffed. "Or everything."

Shaking her head, she finished pulling her hair up. "Who were you talking to?"

I shot her a playful look. "Jealous? Worried I'm moving on? Don't worry, Bocephus Jane St. James. Fuck, that's a mouthful," I laughed, and though she didn't laugh with me, I saw her lips twitching. "I got eyes only for you."

She dramatically rolled her eyes, wrapping her hair into a messy bun. "Of course, until you get your fill of me on Saturday as you keep reminding me, and then off you'll go, spreading your seed."

I pressed my hands into my chest. "Hey, my seed goes right into a condom."

She gave me a dry look. "Wow, I could have gone the rest of my life without hearing that."

Watching as she hobbled to her bag, of course, I got my fill of her ass as my lips spread wide across my face. I really liked her. More-than-a-fuck like, and while I wasn't sure what that meant, or even what I was going to do about that, I felt okay with it. "I was talking to my parents."

She looked over her shoulder at me. Her brows pulled in, and then she nodded. "Oh, that's nice."

Placing my hands back on the boards, I started to swing once more. "Yeah, I was asking my mom for pointers on my jumps. I want the girls to get it today."

Standing up, she crossed her arms and leaned on her good

leg. "Trying to be better than me?"

I nodded. "I wanted to make sure I was up to par."

Her smile fell off, her eyes burning into mine. "I wouldn't have agreed if I didn't think you were up to par."

I shrugged. "Well, maybe I just want to make sure to impress you."

"Why do you care?"

"Because I do," I answered. "I think I've said before that I don't want to let you down."

She didn't say anything. Her eyes were locked into mine, her breathing started to elevate, her breasts moving with the motion in the most erotic way. I wanted so bad for those tits to be in my mouth again. To taste every single inch of her once more, but that would have to wait.

Until Saturday.

But what I didn't notice as I was drinking in every single detail of her was that she was moving toward me, her eyes still locked with mine before her hands rested across mine on the boards. She whispered, "You make it very hard for me to hate you."

Unable to move, my gaze dropped to her plump lips. I whispered back, "That's my plan."

"I figured."

As I watched her eyes, her lips, and her face as she searched my face, my whole body went taut and my cock strained in my shorts. I wanted to close the distance between us and press my mouth to hers, but I had promised to be on my best behavior, so I didn't move. But boy, did my body want hers.

Reaching up, she stroked her thumb along my bottom lip

as her eyes met mine. "I should hate you."

"Why? It takes too much energy." I don't know how I got the words out. "Giving in is so much easier."

Her eyes darkened. "Have you given in?"

I nodded, my head moving like a fucking bobblehead. "From the moment I saw you."

She sucked her lip between her teeth. "I have a secret."

I couldn't breathe. I really couldn't as I moved my mouth into her hand. "I can keep a secret."

She leaned closer and pressed her mouth against her thumb so that slim digit was the only thing between our lips. "Maybe I can't wait for Saturday."

Yup, fuck behaving.

Taking her by the elbow, I pulled her arm down, and her lips fell into mine, her chest pressing to me as I wrapped my arms around her waist and held her tight against me. She pressed her hands against my chest, but I wasn't letting her go yet. I couldn't. When I swept my tongue along her lips, she opened her mouth so our tongues could play in the most stimulating but rewarding way. Pressing my nose into hers, I slid my hands down her back. I grabbed that ass I adored so that I could press my hardness into her soft center.

She gasped against my mouth, and I couldn't help it... I smiled. She drove me absolutely wild. When I pulled back, her eyes fluttered open, and boy, were they dark with lust. Nipping at her bottom lip, I licked it before I whispered, "I don't want to wait."

Swallowing hard, she pushed her hands into my chest, putting unwanted space between us. With a little gleam in her eye and a smile on her face that basically knocked me on my ass, she said, "Well, you're gonna have to."

I almost protested, but then out of the corner of my eye, I saw a parent and child walking toward us. Looking back to Bo, I shook my head. "Unfair."

She pursed her lips, waving me off as she bent down to hug the child.

Needing more than a few minutes, I went to do laps... before I pushed the kid out of the way and then took her coach and fucked her, hard, against the wall.

My mom was pretty laid-back and crazy, but even she would frown on that.

CHAPTER FIFTEEN

BO

"You're a complete idiot."

Staring back at my reflection, I looked great. Sexy, even. Over a cropped black tank was a black lace overlay that reached to midthigh, where it met my maroon shorts. Though I had that stupid boot on one foot, on my other foot was a cute strappy black sandal that wrapped up my leg to my knee. My hair was curled to perfection, trailing down my shoulders to the tops of my breasts. I wore more makeup than I usually did, making my bright-blue eyes even brighter. I was even impressed by them. My lips were a dark maroon color that I had fallen in love with at the store, but as I stared back at my reflection, I couldn't help but shake my head.

"Why are you trying so hard? You know what's going to happen. You'll go out to dinner, he'll fuck you stupid, and then you'll come home. Alone. And be alone because that's what you want. So why? Explain to me why you did this. Are you getting your hopes up? For what? You don't want this. I really thought you learned your lesson."

Turning from the mirror, I put my wallet and lipstick in my clutch. I couldn't believe I was trying so hard. I didn't even realize what I was doing until two hours had passed and I was standing in front of my mirror, but I had done it. I had gotten all gussied up for Gus.

Like a complete dumbass.

As I reached for my phone, my stomach was churning with nervousness, which I didn't understand. There was nothing to be nervous about. Shit, what was wrong with me? This wasn't me. I didn't get nervous around guys anymore. I had no reason to. Guys didn't matter. Or at least that's what I told myself over and over again.

As I went to tuck my phone into my purse, it started to ring with a FaceTime call. It was my mom. Swallowing hard, I answered it, plastering on a big smile as she came into view. "Hey, honey!"

"Hey, Mom. Where you at?" I asked when I noticed she was outside.

"Davis has a game tonight! I told you I'd FaceTime you."

I wanted to groan. God, I was an idiot. I had forgotten. Crap. "That's right. Let me see."

But her brows were pulled together, frustration on her face. "Now, Bo—"

"I'm sorry. I'm very busy, and I forgot. Don't get on me, please."

"He's—"

"Mom, seriously," I warned, shaking my head. "I'm sorry I forgot. Just let me see him."

She didn't want to let me see him. She wanted to punish me just because she could and it's what she always did. I could see it all over her face. But then my phone screen filled with twenty little boys on the ice.

I had no clue which one was Davis. "Which number?" I asked.

"Sixty-two."

When I saw him, my chest warmed with emotion. He was the smallest out there and couldn't skate a lick. "Is he the youngest out there?"

"Yeah. He doesn't turn five until next month."

I knew that, but I couldn't help smiling. He was so little. "He looks good."

"I'll let him know you said that."

I didn't say anything as I watched him for a moment. I wondered if he would care what I had to say. I hadn't been around for much of his life. I was busy being a teenager and then an adult before moving out to Malibu to try to actually pick up the pieces and do something with my life. Instead of wallowing in self-pity. Although, by the way I was dressed and the way I was feeling, I was pretty sure I was heading right back to that pity party if I didn't get control.

Feelings... They were hard.

Doing things I didn't authorize.

When Davis got knocked over, I hissed out a breath. "Poor guy."

"He's a tough one."

"Didn't expect anything less from two great parents. He's a lucky kid."

"He is," she agreed, but I could hear the annoyance in her voice. "Well, I'll let you go. I'm sure you're busy."

As she came back on the screen, I shrugged. "I guess so."

"Yeah," she said, and then the line went dead.

Well, if I wasn't feeling like shit before, I sure was now. If I forgot for just a second what a guy like Gus Persson could do, that call reminded me. I didn't want to become the girl I used to be, and I was starting to forget that. Gus was cracking me. He was adorable and nice, which weren't words I thought I'd ever use for Gus Persson, but it was true. He was really sweet, and that scared me. I liked that about him. I needed him to go back to being obnoxious so I would get over this little crush that was developing.

"Just get through tonight," I told myself. "After this, you don't have to see him anymore. Get some great ass and walk away. Bo, you got this. No need to worry."

I was completely right. It wasn't like I would see him again. Maybe at the games, but he wouldn't talk to me. One and done. That was his mantra, so surely he would stick by it. He'd blow me off before I could even have any second thoughts about it.

"You're totally good, St. James. No biggie. Go enjoy that sexy ass and then walk away like the big girl you are."

Looking back at the mirror, I shot myself two thumbs up. "You sexy bitch, you."

Turning from the mirror, I found Lizzy on the couch, her legs over the arm rest and her head slightly hanging off. Looking over at me, she scoffed. "You know I can hear you, right?"

I blushed deep red, and before I could say anything, she laughed.

"And you're totally gonna get caught up once you get a look at that cock. I heard it is pretty damn legendary."

It was.

But since I still hadn't told her I had seen it or felt that legendary cock inside me, I rolled my eyes. But it was hard to ignore the flutter in my stomach. Stupid stomach. Stupid Gus. Stupid legendary cock. Swallowing hard, I waved her off before tucking my clutch under my arm. "I'll be fine. One and done, right?"

She laughed once more, shaking her head, her brown mane falling off the couch some. "I don't know, Bo. He seems to be digging you."

I was worried she was gonna say that.

But before I could come up with some kind of excuse why that would never happen, that she was delusional, there was a frantic knock at the door.

Lizzy giggled. "He's really ready to pound ya."

Glancing back at her, I made a *pfft* sound as I reached for the door. When I opened it, I cried out in shock.

Because standing on my doorstep was Gus.

Blood dripped like mad from his hand, and there was a pitiful-looking dog under his arm.

"Gus!"

He shook his head, panic in his eyes. "I had to save her!"

CHAPTER SIXTEEN

GUS

Right back to where I was used to being.

On a gurney.

But unlike where my mom or dad would sit, Bo was beside me and a doctor stood at the end of the bed. I moved my good hand as I spoke. "The poor girl dog was being attacked by three other big dogs. I thought if I went up, made a few loud noises, I'd scare them and they'd run away, but obviously, I was wrong."

I held my hand up for the example that I probably didn't have to give but did anyway. The doctor did not appear to find me amusing. I felt Bo's gaze on me. When I glanced over at her, she was looking at me like I was insane.

Maybe I was.

But that sweet girl dog was gorgeous, and I couldn't let her be treated like that.

Clearing his throat, the doctor asked, "So you tried to separate them?"

I threw my good hand up. "Yeah. I mean, they were big! She was all hollering and crying. I couldn't just ignore it. I had to save her."

The doctor blinked once more, total disbelief on his face.

"So you risked getting rabies to save a homeless dog from being attacked?"

"We don't know she was a homeless dog," I corrected. "She is so sweet, and I couldn't tell if she had a collar. It wasn't a fair fight! I couldn't stand by and let her get torn to shreds by three big old dogs. It was truly sad, and I had no choice—"

"You could have let dogs be dogs."

I shook my head. Why was I being scrutinized here? "I couldn't. I felt awful, and I didn't think twice. I had to save her. Anyone would have stopped them."

"I wouldn't have," the doctor corrected. "They could have seriously injured you—torn ligaments, nerve damage. You're lucky you only have a few bites and need just a couple of stitches. It could have been much worse. You could develop an infection, you could lose your hand, or even worse, die."

I waved him off. "Please. I'm good. I got bitten like twice. I was fine until they got my hand. I was kicking like a ninja, and I got her up in my arms before she got hurt more."

This time, it was the doctor throwing his hands out toward me. "What if she had bitten you?"

I shook my head. "Nah, she loves me."

More blinking from the doctor as Bo giggled beside me.

I shot her a wink before I looked back at the doctor. "What if it was your dog? Would you want her to suffer like that when some guy could have jumped in and helped her?"

Exhaling hard, the doctor wrote in his chart without even looking at me.

Asshole.

He was older, though, and didn't understand I was trying

to impress the hottie beside me. And man, did she look good tonight. I mean, I thought she was fine all the time, but tonight, whoowee. With tight shorts, a little belly showing, and those tits that were mouthwatering, it was almost unfair that our date was starting in an ER. I wanted to show her off to everyone. I wanted to honestly just sit there and stare at her. Her eyes were darker, probably from the makeup, but I sort of liked it. I really loved her lips, though. They were a dark red and so damn plump. I wanted to smear that lipstick with my mouth, eat away every bit of the color and devour every inch of her.

But before I could, the doctor was speaking once more. "Okay, we're going to run some antibiotics through you, and then you can go. We've contacted your team doctor. That's protocol. If he wants to see you, you'll have to wait for him."

Well, that sucked. "So you're saying I'll be here a bit?"

"At least another three hours. If you're lucky."

I groaned slightly as he in return rolled his eyes and left. Bo was watching me. "So, I suck."

She shrugged, shaking her head. "You don't."

"I do. I ruined a perfectly good evening with a super-hot chick."

Her face filled with color as she looked away, swallowing hard. "It's fine. You saved a dog."

I smiled. "You don't think I'm dumb?"

She laughed a little. "Dumb, no. But crazy, yes. I wouldn't have the balls to do such a thing. You could have lost your hand."

I shrugged. "If that's the way it would have played out, then that's that."

MISADVENTURES WITH A ROOKIE

Her gaze narrowed as she looked over at me. "It's your career though, everything you've worked for."

"Yeah, but if it wasn't meant to be, it wasn't meant to be. I live in the now. I work my ass off in the hopes that I'll be rewarded, but nothing is promised. Everything can change like that." Snapping my fingers for emphasis, I held her gaze. "I probably should have thought that through before I saved the dog, but if I worried so much about every move, I'd be full of anxiety. I don't want that. I want to be happy."

She blinked a few times and then slowly shook her head. "It's like you're out to prove every single thing I assumed about you wrong."

My grin grew, and I shot her a wink. "Ah, you're onto me."

The curtain opened, and in came a nurse to start my antibiotics. As she was hooking everything up, I asked, "Hey, can I eat?"

She nodded. "Of course."

"Cool, thanks," I said before looking back over to Bo. She was sitting straight up, her hands in her lap as she moved her fingers along one another. She was picking at her nail polish, and I loved that I was driving her crazy. "Hey, you don't have to stay if you don't want to."

She smiled, slowly lifting her shoulder. "I want to."

Flashing a grin, I nodded. "Cool. Let's order some food, then."

"That sounds great. I'm starving."

"So am I," I decided as I pulled my phone out, but before I could suggest something, the doctor popped his head in.

"Hey, your team doctor is coming in, so it's going to be a

bit."

"Awesome." It sucked that I was stuck in the ER, but glancing over at Bo, her lips glistening in the horrible hospital lights, I couldn't think of a better person I'd rather share the time with. "Pizza or noodles?"

"Pizza."

I nodded in agreement. "A girl after my own heart."

I didn't miss the look on her face, probably because she thought it was a line.

But the more time I spent with Bo St. James, the more I realized the words were true.

And the funny thing was, she wasn't even trying.

She was just being her.

♦ ♦ ♦ ♦

"No way."

I grinned, catching the cheese that was trying to escape from my pizza. "No really. They took all my clothes and froze them to the ice."

She sputtered with laughter, covering her mouth with one hand as she held her slice with the other. "What did you do?"

"What any confident and hung man would do."

"Jesus," she groaned.

I cracked up and continued. "As I was saying, I went out there, naked as the day I was born, but of course, a lot more hung."

She nodded, holding her hand out. "Of course."

I held back more laughter. "I peeled my clothes off the ice, put my boxers on, and left."

She was holding her belly, giggling hard. "You weren't even the least bit embarrassed?"

I thought that over for a moment. I'd been only sixteen and already the best in town. Everyone thought I pissed gold, and I wasn't going to correct them. Nor was I going to allow my team to try to bring me down from my high. "Nope, but let me tell you, my balls stuck to those shorts, and boy, did that hurt."

More laughter, and I couldn't hold back, joining in with her as she leaned back in her seat, shaking her head. "I am floored. I would have been so embarrassed!"

"Eh, I learned very early that other people's thoughts of me can't bring me down. Only I can."

Her light mood eased a bit as she eyed me. "Yeah?"

"Oh, yeah." I took a bite of pizza and talked around it. "I was the best early on, and really fast. I had that raw natural talent people just want so bad. With that comes the nasty jealousy. Everyone hated me. They hated my mom and soon my dad, when he started coming around, especially since he was loaded."

She held up her hand, confusion evident on her beautiful features. "Huh?"

I took another bite. "Huh, what?"

"Your dad 'came around'? I'm confused. Back up a bit."

I grinned. "No way. That's my deep dark secret!"

Her face lit up. "Not fair! You have to tell me."

"I don't have to tell you anything," I shot back.

Her eyes narrowed, and she pointed a finger at me. "I have been sitting here with you—"

"Um, excuse me, Bocephus, but I sat with you."

"After you broke my ankle!"

"Beside the point. I sat with you, and I bought you food."

She bubbled with laugher. "I don't care! Tell me your 'deep dark secret'! I know darn well it isn't!"

I held her gaze. "It is!"

"Please. You're an open book."

She wasn't wrong, but I wanted to know more about her. This was an opportunity to get her to open up, even if I wasn't really giving her personal info. "Either way," I said. "I'll give you some if you give me some."

Her eyes turned to storm clouds, her cheeks dusting with color. The flush trailed along her throat, and within seconds, I was hotter than hot. I couldn't see straight. I wasn't even sure how those words and those eyes brought on the kind of lust that was rattling me at that moment, but it was happening.

I wanted her.

Bad.

"You make everything dirty," she exclaimed.

I laughed out loud. "Me? That's all you! You're giving me the sex eyes."

She sputtered, shaking her head. "I am not!"

"You are. Your face turns red and then your neck, and I know those tits are all red and splotchy! It isn't fair."

More giggling as she waved her hand. "You are insane."

"Maybe," I said with a shrug, mostly to calm myself. I couldn't take her here. I knew I couldn't. Not with the team doctor coming to check me out. Chet ran his mouth a lot. Lived for the drama, and I didn't need people knowing I was caught banging an ice girl at the ER. Not because I would be

MISADVENTURES WITH A ROOKIE

embarrassed, but I was sure Bo would be, and I couldn't have that. "But nonetheless, you gotta give something up if I'm going to."

She eyed me, her eyes swirling with all things hot as she shook her head. "Fine."

"Fine?"

"Fine," she answered before she blew out a breath. "I'm sure I'll regret it though."

"No, you'll love it."

She shook her head and reached for another piece. She liked to eat, and I loved it. Usually girls I went to dinner with ate absolutely nothing, which I thought was bullshit. Especially when they sucked down two bottles of wine. Sex with a drunk chick wasn't fun. I was all for her eating. Plus, I loved the way her mouth moved when she did.

"Can you stop staring at me?" She leaned back and crossed her legs. "And tell me about your family, please?"

I wasn't feeling the least bit guilty. "Maybe I love staring at you."

She flushed. "Gus."

"Bo."

She set me with a look as she chewed. "Start talking, or I'm zipping my lips."

I could have fought with her on that, I really would have liked to, but instead I reached for another piece and slathered it in ranch before I took a bite. "Okay, so," I started before I chewed and swallowed. "My mom got knocked up at like fifteen, maybe? By my dad."

She widened her eyes. "Oh. I thought they were married

and stuff like that."

I laughed. "Oh God, no. I think my mom wished that was how it played out because she didn't even like my dad at first. They were just friends who got drunk at a street party back home and then afterward they found themselves banging."

She tried to hold in her laughter but couldn't. "She told you that?"

I nodded. "Yeah, they're young and sometimes treat me like a friend instead of their kid."

"Oh."

"Yeah, but at the same time, I like it because they understand me, I guess."

She thought that over. "Yeah, I can see that."

I smiled. "But yeah, Dad knocked up Mom, and since his family was so well-off, old money—and I mean *old*—they sent him off to boarding school and tried to pay my mom off to get an abortion. She wouldn't, which pissed my grandparents off, and they kicked her out. So she went to stay with my great-aunt and somehow raised me."

She looked down at her feet. "Wow, she must be one hell of a woman."

"She's something," I said with a grin. "But my dad came back when I was six-ish, maybe right around my sixth birthday. I don't remember, but he bought me an Xbox, and I thought he was one cool dude. My mom hated him, for obvious reasons. He claimed he wanted to be in my life and hers, and she kicked him to the curb. That went on for about a year, but he was there for me. At every game, cheering me on, and he bought me whatever I needed for the ice and off the ice. He bought her things, helped fix up our trailer since she wouldn't let him buy her a house. He was trying so damn hard, and I felt bad for him when she would reject him and slam the door in his face."

A smile played on her face as I laughed.

"But finally, he somehow convinced her to give him a chance, and they got married the next week."

She gasped. "The next week!"

"Yeah, I guess the sex was awesome 'cause I wasn't allowed to leave my boy Jack's house for a whole weekend." I laughed at the memory. "But once they were married, it was awesome. We were a family, and my mom didn't stress about money. She did her thing, she still worked, but she was happier. My dad takes credit for that, and I guess he should because I was happier too. She didn't cry anymore, so that was nice."

"Wow," she said softly. "That's amazing." But as she said the words, it didn't seem like she was thinking about them. It was like she was in her own world, her eyes glazing over as she looked down at her hands. She inhaled hard as she scraped the cheese off the crust. Letting it out slowly, she shook her head, and I wanted to know so bad what she was thinking. But I knew she wouldn't tell me.

"Yeah, so while you want to believe I was some stuck-up rich kid, I was, but only from like eight and on," I teased.

She laughed, though it didn't reach her eyes.

"No silver spoon, I guess," she muttered.

"Nope. I never got to use it, but my grandmom says I have one, which is cool. I've never seen it."

She giggled, shaking her head. "I guess I owe you an apology."

I scoffed. "Please, don't. You didn't know me."

"I didn't." The words came out in a whisper. My fiery ice girl showing a soft side.

"And now that you do, please don't rush to fall in love with me. Let's go slow."

That made her laugh out loud. I leaned back and threw the crust in the box as I watched her.

"You're insufferable."

"But hot," I reminded her, though I didn't think she needed the reminder.

She tossed her crust into the box before picking a slice of pepperoni off another piece.

"Your turn," I pressed. "Tell me something, Bocephus, that no one else knows."

The look of panic that filled her eyes as she glanced up at me was something I would never forget.

But then, I was finding that there were a lot of things about Bo that were hard to forget.

CHAPTER SEVENTEEN

BO

I swear the pepperoni I just threw in my mouth was lodged in my throat. Between the revelation about his parents that rattled my soul and the fact that it was becoming very hard to hate this guy, I felt like I was having a small panic attack. As I worked to dislodge it, I tried to come up with anything that would count as a deep dark secret—but not my real one. Though his family history wasn't really a secret, I knew I couldn't come out with something silly like I don't like carrots! He'd call me on it within seconds. But I couldn't tell him my real story.

I just couldn't.

But even though I was nowhere near ready to trust him, I admit I felt like things were shifting for us. Even against my better judgment, I couldn't ignore the fact that I liked the person I was getting to know. Would it last? No, he'd do something, or better yet, he'd be gone before I could ever utter the words that scared the living shit out of me. Not that I was thinking them, but it was hard to ignore the fact that I could actually feel those for him. Even if I was idiot for it—because, *hello*, I had a fucked-up history and had sworn off men—as

I sat there looking at him, I couldn't shake the feeling that something real could happen. That alone should have had me hightailing it out of there. He could find a ride home. His buddy, Maxy, could come.

But the thing was, I didn't want him to.

I wanted to be the one to take Gus home.

Man... What the hell was I doing?

Exhaling hard after choking a bit more, I looked over at him and shrugged. "I have no secrets."

He laughed out loud. "You're a liar."

"I am not."

"You are," he said simply, reaching for his pop. He took a long swig and then pointed it toward me. "You have to tell me, I told you mine."

I set him with a look. "So no one knows that about your parents?"

He shrugged. "I mean, my whole town does, but that's only because they talk too damn much."

I wanted to laugh, but I didn't. I knew all about small towns, I'd been the high topic around mine. Which was the main reason I'd wanted to leave so bad. Shrugging, I picked up a discarded crust out of the box and moved my fingers along the dry edges, pricking myself with the hard parts. "So it isn't a secret."

"Sure it is. I don't tell everyone."

I glanced over at him, and he was watching me with those deep-green eyes, a grin playing on his lips. I liked when he smiled like that. It was a little quirk that gave him a small dimple right by his lips. It was adorable and breathtaking.

Stupid dimple.

I looked away, shrugging hard as I blew out a breath. "I really don't know what you want to know."

"Everything," he said without even holding back.

I looked up quickly, a tremor in my chest at the word. "Everything?"

"Everything," he said simply. "But a deep dark secret is a good start. I mean, we got nothing but time, Bocephus, so hit me with it."

"Can you please stop calling me that?"

He shook his head. "No way. It's growing on me." He flashed me a big grin, and I couldn't help it. I smiled back. "Plus, I like the flush that fills your cheeks and the annoying little twitch you get in your nose."

I felt the blush fill my face as I held his gaze. "You annoy me."

He chuckled. "Ah, you like it."

I did. A lot.

Crap.

"No, I don't," I said defensively.

He gave me a look that meant he didn't believe me one bit. "Stop stalling. Tell me something, BJSJ."

"Jesus, you and all these names for me."

He shrugged. "You give me a lot to work with."

My heart was pounding, and sweat was gathering at the base of my neck and along my ears. Oh my God! "I sweat behind my ears!"

One brow rose. "Huh?"

"That's my secret. I sweat behind my ears."

"You sweat behind your ears?"

"Yes, in gross amounts when I'm nervous." I almost stopped sweating I was so relieved I'd come up with something—anything—that might fill the expectation between us.

He eyed me. "Are you sweating now?"

"Yes."

"I don't believe you."

I leaned toward him, moving my hair. "Feel."

He looked a little too happy about testing my secret. He leaned toward me, running his fingers along the back of my ear. His face was closer than it needed to be, but I didn't mind. Especially when his eyes met mine. "That is disgusting."

"I know!" I went to move away, but then his hand gathered my hair and pulled me closer.

"But having you this close, I don't care."

His eyes were dark and reflected my own naughty thoughts. Swallowing hard, I looked at his lips. He smelled like a dream, and this close, I could see that he hadn't shaved. God, he was gorgeous. "I don't hate it."

His lips quirked as his nose moved along mine, his gaze meeting mine. "But, Bo..."

Getting lost in his eyes, I whispered, "Yeah?"

"I know damn well that the sweat behind your ears isn't your secret. So you should just come out with the real stuff."

He pulled back, and I glared, my heart in my throat as I gasped for breath. I was hot all over, and damn it, I wanted those lips on mine! They were so scrumptious, so thick, and ugh! "You are mean."

He shrugged. "Some would agree, but that doesn't matter at this moment. All that matters is your secret."

"There is nothing to tell," I tried again, but he was already shaking his head.

"Are you really gonna go back on your promise?"

He crossed his arms and, to my surprise, pouted. I couldn't help myself. I giggled. He looked so pathetic, his face all scrunched up and his eyes holding mine in complete frustration. "I thought we were getting to know each other. Guess you are just using me for sex."

There was no holding in my laughter that time. I almost fell out of my chair. I was laughing so hard as I shook my head. "I'm sorry, you got that all wrong. You're using me."

He feigned a pain in his heart. "Never."

I sputtered with more laughter as I leaned back in my seat, crossing my legs as I watched him pout some more. "How do you even know I have a secret?"

"'Cause I heard you," he shot back to me, though he wouldn't look at me.

My brows pulled together. "Huh?"

He looked over at me then. "That night at the box, the chicks you were with, they asked you about college, and you deflected. I knew there was more there, and I want to know about it."

My face scrunched up in disbelief. "You were listening?"

He scoffed. "Duh." Again my heart was doing a wild jig in my chest as he held my gaze, waiting for the truth. "Why didn't you go to college when you got that full ride?"

I felt like something was in my throat, lodged so I couldn't speak. Nothing was working. I was almost frozen.

When he reached out, taking my hand in his, he laced our fingers together. His eyes burned into mine. "I would never tell anyone."

I swallowed hard, gazing into his emerald depth as he whispered, "I know you'd kill me if I did."

I smiled, laughter bubbling in my chest as I looked down at our hands. "It doesn't matter. It's all in the past."

He shrugged. "Sure. But I want to know."

"Why?"

"I think it's gonna open up who you are."

Glancing down at our hands, I covered them with my other and inhaled hard. Did I want him to know who I was? Why did he want to know? Why was this so damn hard? I was supposed to have wild sex and leave...yet, here I was...not wanting to leave. And seriously considering opening up to the one guy I swore I'd never get involved with.

Before I could even mutter a word, the curtain opened and a guy dressed in a Suns T-shirt and jeans came in. It was Chet McPherance, the team doctor. With his lips pursed, Chet rolled his eyes. "Really, Persson?"

Gus laughed as he let go of my hand. "What? I'm good."

He came toward the bed, and I cleared away the pizza box, my heart still pounding in my chest. I had worked a bit with Chet—not much, but I'd seen him enough in passing to know his face.

He unwrapped Gus's hand and examined the stitches and wounds. "You could have lost your hand."

"I'm fine."

"Was the dog worth it?"

He nodded proudly, and my heart may have skipped a beat. "She's a beauty for sure."

"Well, there is that. You know I love dogs."

"I do too," he said, flinching a bit while Chet put the bandages back on.

"Everything looks fine, but you can't play tomorrow."

Pure rage filled Gus's features. I was so used to his playful way that his angry side scared the shit out of me. "What the hell do you mean? I'm fine! Dude, come on, I can't sit out."

"Persson, I can't let this get infected being in your gloves. At least if you sit out a night, you have four days of healing."

"I'll get a new pair!"

"It doesn't matter. You sweat in your gloves. That can't sit on that wound! You need a couple nights off."

"That's bullshit. Wrap it with cellophane or something!"

But Chet was shaking his head. "Sorry, Persson. You're sitting out tomorrow." He tapped Gus's knee and then reached for the chart. "You can go home as soon as the ER doctor releases ya. Have a good night."

He left without waiting for Gus to answer, probably because it was apparent that Gus was pissed as fuck.

I walked to the bed and leaned my hip against it. "I'm sorry."

He shrugged. "It is what it is. Just fucking sucks."

"I know," I agreed.

"I can't sit out when I want to go to the Tornadoes, you know?"

"Yeah, I hear you. But they are already seeing you. You're

doing so great."

"Yeah, but I wanted to play more. Fuck."

I inhaled hard and really didn't know what to say. When he reached up, taking my hand with his good one, I met his gaze as he shrugged. "Oh well, at least I got to be with you."

That stupid heart of mine skipped a stupid beat once more. "I'm sure you'd rather play than hang with me."

"I want both," he said, and then he kissed the side of my hand. "I'm ready to get out of here."

"Me too."

He glanced up at me and smiled, but that wasn't what had me gasping for breath. No, it was the pure unadulterated lust in his eyes that consumed me from the top of my head to the bottom of my feet. How he could go from upset to horny in two seconds was beyond me, but then...I was feeling the exact same thing. I wanted him, desperately.

Pursing his lips up at me, he blew me a kiss before he said, "Don't worry. We'll be naked soon enough."

That should have pleased me. It should have gotten my engines burning, but it didn't.

It saddened me.

Because that meant this would be over soon.

Oh, I was in so much trouble.

CHAPTER EIGHTEEN

GUS

"Man, it's going to be a boring game tomorrow."

I glanced over at Bo. The windows of her Jeep were down. The breeze blew her hair everywhere. I expected her to pull those red locks up, but she didn't. She drove, oblivious to the strands tangling against her face. She looked like one of the babes I liked checking out. She wasn't tanned like typical eye candy on the beach. I was pretty sure she'd turn into a lobster if she went outside. Her cheeks were red from the fresh air, but then they had been like that all night.

And what a night. I thought it was going to be awful. Sitting in an ER was never the best time, but being there with her was. I loved listening to her laugh. I was bummed that I wasn't going to play tomorrow, but the more I thought about it, the more I knew the doctor was right. I was just glad the dog, Sweetie, was okay. In the time it took me to get out of the ER, Maxy had named her and taken her to the vet. I was kind of pissed I didn't get to name her, but at the same time, I would have named her something worse than he had.

Either way, the night wasn't a total loss, and it wasn't even over yet.

"Yeah, it sucks, but I don't want to lose my hand," I said with a small laugh.

She smiled over at me, nodding. "Yeah, that would suck."

"Exactly. How could I grab your ass or tits with only one hand?"

Rolling her eyes, she looked back at the road. "No one said you're touching either my ass or my tits."

I scoffed. "You wouldn't stop me. Especially if I went after those naughty bits with my mouth."

She squirmed in her seat, and I fought back my laughter.

"Now, you never said mouth. You said hands." She smiled as she glanced back at the road. "So, Sweetie?"

I exhaled hard. "Apparently. I would have called her Smooches or something, so it's good he named her."

She giggled. "Really? I thought you'd name her Puck or something hockey-ish."

I shook my head. "No way. She's too pretty. You'll have to come over and meet her. You didn't get a good look at her, and Max gave her a bath, apparently."

She inhaled sharply as she turned. "He's been busy."

"Yep. He has time. He isn't getting laid right now."

Her faced scrunched up as she laughed. "How do you know that? Wait, you guys admit that to each other?"

I scoffed and waved her off. "No, but his girlfriend is back home. She's waiting to see where he gets called up. There is talk he'll get traded soon, so they're waiting, and since he isn't the cheating type, he isn't having sex, except of the phone variety. FYI, she's loud."

I expected her to laugh—I mean, that was funny—but she

135

didn't. "Do you expect him to cheat?"

Of course that was what she heard out of that whole thing. "No, I'm just pointing out why he isn't getting laid."

"Oh."

"He loves the girl, a lot, and it's cute, I guess."

"You guess," she commented, very sassy-like.

I eyed her. "You're setting me up for failure here, Bocephus."

She scoffed. "You're the one talking."

I glared at her. "You're trying to use my words against me so you can figure a way out of this."

She stopped the car. "Out of this?" She scowled at me.

We were parked outside her apartment.

"Yes, this." I said. "Don't ask me *what* this, but *this*."

She rolled her eyes. "That makes a lot of sense."

I stayed in the car a few seconds longer so I could watch her get out and check out her ass. Then I followed close behind. As she led the way up the stairs, neither of us said anything. I wasn't sure if it was because we both were anticipating what was about to happen in her room or if she was still pissed. Either way, I was on edge, and my cock was hard as fuck. Especially after the show she made of jiggling her ass as she climbed an endless number of stairs.

Finally we reached the door, and she fished for her keys. "Lizzy isn't home."

I came up behind her, wrapping my arms around her waist and nuzzling my nose in her hair. "Good. Means you can scream as loud as you want."

She didn't acknowledge me, just opened the door and

went inside. Before I could make it in, she stopped and looked at me. She blocked my entry by leaning her hip against the doorframe.

She wasn't going to let me in!

"Really?"

"Gus—"

"You aren't going to let me in because of that comment?"

Holding my gaze, she slowly shook her head. "Actually, no, that's not it." I drank in her face, the uncertainty in her eyes and flush that began at her neck, running down her chest. "Listen, it's actually more."

I waited as she just stood there staring me down. "And that is?"

She exhaled hard, her face filling with flush as she shook her head. "This is so stupid—"

"It's not stupid if you feel it. Just tell me, what's wrong? I thought we were banging."

She held her hand up to me and nodded. "That. That's all you want, and somehow, I've, sorta, kinda, well... I started... Fucking hell, I kinda don't hate you anymore."

I curved my lips in a knowing smile as she let out a long, frustrated breath.

"And if I let you in and take you to bed and do all the naughty shit I dream of doing with you, I don't think I would be able to handle you ignoring me and blowing me off, like I know you will once you get what you want. What I want too. I've been really hurt, Gus, like bone-deep hurt, and I feel like you could do that to me. And I know I'm being pathetic, but honestly, I can't. You're too much of a distraction. At least this way, you walking one way, me walking the other way, there are no hard feelings."

There was so much to say. It was all there, but I was wrung tight, and all I could do was stare at her.

"See? Now I've freaked you out. Go on, run away, Gus the Bus. I'm sure you won't go to bed alone. Thanks for a great night. Hope your hand gets better."

She tried to shut the door, but I reached out and stopped her. She looked from the door back to me. "First, I don't want anyone else in my bed but you." Pushing the door open, I went toe-to-toe with her, capturing her sweet face in my good hand. I ran my thumb along her lip, lost in those blue eyes that rattled me so deeply. "Second, who said anything about blowing you off or ignoring you?"

She was breathless, her pupils dilating as she gasped for breath. "Everyone knows that Gus the Bus hits and runs."

"Maybe because I haven't met anyone to station up at," I said softly. When her lips curved, I chuckled. "Damn, that was corny."

"So damn corny." She laughed.

I inhaled hard, wrapping my bad arm around her and bringing her in closer. "But really, Bo, I didn't intend on not seeing you after tonight."

She didn't believe me. I could see it in her eyes. Hell, I almost couldn't believe I said it myself, but I meant it.

"I've been told that before."

Moving my hand into her hair, I ran my thumb along her eyebrow and smiled down at her. "But you haven't met someone like me."

She laughed slightly. "He was everything like you, only you're hotter."

"Well, at least I have that." I grinned. "I think you should just let it happen. We can think about the other stuff later."

She bit her lip, and a breath rushed out of her as she slowly shook her head. "I can't do that. Just in the time I've known you and sorta not hated you, I've been distracted with thoughts of getting you naked. If I do take you to my bedroom and let it happen, then that's it, I'm gonna be crushed. I can't be that girl again, Gus. I was pathetic. I mean, you don't even know. I was..." She struggled with the words. "I made a bad decision, and I can't let it happen again. I know the warning signs, and you are one huge warning sign."

No one had ever called me that before. I have been called a lot, but never a warning sign. I understood what she was saying. She'd been hurt before. I got it. She was obviously still bitter. But it was time to get it on with someone else and fucking enjoy it. But that wasn't the way Bo thought. She saw long term, she saw forever, the future, while I was living for the now. Clearing my throat, I nodded. "I completely respect what you're saying, but I really want you."

Her face broke into a wide smile. "I really want you. But there is no guarantee that you'll call me tomorrow, which scares me."

"What if I stay and I don't leave until tomorrow?" I suggested.

"Your new dog?" She laughed.

"Oh yeah, I do have to go home to see her and make sure she's good," I said, and then I nodded, moving my nose along hers. "I can guarantee you I'll call tomorrow."

She slowly moved out of my arms, shaking her head. "Again, I've heard that one."

At that moment, I decided I wanted to kill the fucker who had hurt her. I wanted to say something, some line, though I wasn't sure what. I hadn't had a girl reject me as hard as Bo was, and I think that was what was holding me up. Women loved me. I was irresistible. Yet I understood what she was saying. I got it... I just didn't like it. When my phone vibrated in my pocket, probably with an email, a light bulb went off in my head. Reaching into my pocket, I pulled out my phone and held it out to her.

She looked down at it and then back at me as I said, "Take it. My life is in this electronic device, and when I come back for you, I'll pick it up."

She blinked. "What?"

"You said you need a guarantee. Here it is," I said, reaching for her arms the best I could with my bad hand before placing my phone in her hand. "It's unlocked. I have nothing to hide. I think there are some videos, so get some popcorn and watch the show. If you're still moving once I'm done with you."

She gasped as she glanced back up at me. "You're serious?"

I nodded. "I know for a fact Sweetie and I are going to come by tomorrow to go hang out on the beach with you. You can give it to me then." She was speechless, just the way I liked her. Reaching for her by cupping the back of her neck, I brought her in, our mouths so close that all I had to do was dip a little and I'd be kissing her, but I wanted to hear her consent.

"Let me take you to bed, Bocephus Jane St. James."

She let out a long breath, her eyes burning into mine as she rested her hands against my chest. The top of my phone, still clenched in her fist, dug into my pec, but I wasn't moving. I was trapped by her beautiful gaze. Her seductive lips.

Her.

All of her.

Bo.

Or that long-ass name she had, either way.

"I thought you just take what you want?" she asked breathlessly.

"You're right, I do. But with you, I want you to want to give it to me. It means more that way."

As the silence stretched between us, I wasn't sure what was happening.

But there was no stopping it.

CHAPTER NINETEEN

BO

I couldn't say no if I'd wanted.

Thank God I didn't have to.

Crashing my mouth to his, I dropped his phone and slid my fingers into his hair. As we kissed, we moved into the apartment. The door slammed shut as his fingers bit into the small of my back. He clung to me, my center pressed against his thick, hard cock. Gasping against his mouth, I couldn't believe I had given in, but then, who was I kidding? I tried. I really did. It just didn't work.

I wanted him.

And my heart, well, it would just have to wait and see what happened.

"You are so fucking beautiful," he said as we pulled apart.

If it was a line, I didn't care. I felt fucking beautiful. Reaching for his hand, I bit into my bottom lip as I wobbled backward, the boot on my foot making my sexy seductive walk a little harder than I was used to. He drank me in, his eyes traveling over my body as he took hold of his cock through his shorts. He shook his head. "I'm gonna blow right here."

"Don't," I whispered. I opened my bedroom door and

brought him inside.

He reached for me and pulled my tank over my body. "Fucking hell. No bra? You should have told me that earlier," he groaned, taking my right breast in his hand. "This sucks with one hand. When I'm healed, I need a redo with these babies."

A giggle escaped my lips. He brought me to bed, sitting down before drawing me into his lap. His cock was so hard. Taking my breast in his hand, he nibbled at my nipple, running his tongue along it, taking his time tasting my whole breast. I expected this to be fast, but apparently, I was very wrong.

His mouth still hot against my nipple, he traced the outside of my pussy through my shorts with his fingers. I was sure he could feel that I was dripping wet. I was hot everywhere. My breathing was out of control. He bit into my tit, and I threw my head back. I cried out as he ran his fingers up and down my pussy lips through my shorts.

"Gus, stop. Let me take them off."

He shook his head against my nipple. "No."

Oh fuck, I was going to die.

I arched into his hand and threw my head back as he pressed his fingers into my clit, flicking his tongue along my nipple with feverous need. When he stopped, I moaned, but then he drew my back to his chest before reaching inside my shorts. He cupped my pussy with his strong fingers. "Fuck, you're so wet."

I couldn't speak. I couldn't even breathe. I let my head fall back on his shoulder as he swirled his fingers inside my lips. When he found my clit, he rubbed it ever so slowly. "I want to suck you in my mouth, Bo. This right here," he said, pressing his finger against my clit.

I gasped and arched toward him.

"I want it in my mouth," he demanded. "Now."

Before I could even agree, he pushed me back onto the bed and tried to rip my shorts off. They snagged on my boot. He tried to free them, but it was no use—they stuck to the Velcro. "This boot is going to be the death of me." He laughed as he freed the shorts.

All I could do was giggle. It was silly and stupid, but it was hot. I was exposed and ready for him, but he stopped, trailing kisses up my leg as he undid my other shoe. "I want you completely naked, except for good ole bootie, there."

I laughed as he threw my shoe to the ground before kissing his way back up my leg, thigh, and then around my pussy. Moving a finger around my lips, he looked up at me as my whole body shook with need. "Do the curtains match the drapes?"

I shot him a look. "Really?"

He chuckled. "I have to know. Tell me. No fair—you shave!"

I rolled my eyes. "I'm not telling you."

He took that as a challenge before he slowly lowered his mouth to me. "Yet."

Fuck, I was already about to come and he hadn't even touched me yet. But when he did, oh Lord, everything just stopped. He traced my lips with his tongue and, when he found it, loved my clit with the patience of a saint. I was shaking, my whole body in fits as he devoured my pussy, licking every inch of it. When he started to fuck me with his tongue, I lifted my legs over his shoulders, careful not to kick him with that stupid boot. Not that I thought he would notice. He was consuming me. Not leaving a single inch of me untasted. He slid his fingers inside me, fucking me fast and hard, his mouth still working my clit. Both movements had me undone within seconds. His name fell from my lips in sounds I had never heard myself make before.

He lifted his head before kissing my belly and then my chest. He found my breast and settled his weight on top of me. I welcomed the feel of him. He felt amazing. When his mouth met mine, our slow, sensual kisses left me breathless. When he pulled back, his hands framed my face, his bad hand hard against my face, but I didn't care. I was too lost in his eyes.

A little grin set on his lips as he traced my lips with his finger. "You screamed my name," he sang, and I rolled my eyes.

"Oh shut it. What are you waiting for? Can't get it up?" I teased, even though I could feel him rock hard against my thigh.

He scoffed, shaking his head. "If I take you right now, I'll embarrass myself."

"Maybe I want that." I watched his eyes turn dark as he nibbled at my lip. "Maybe I want you vulnerable for once."

"You will be the death of me, Bo."

Sitting up on his haunches, he took off his shirt. His toned muscles were just unfair. He was ripped. Abs, pecs—muscles that I hadn't even seen before were defined in his chest and ribs. It was disgustingly gorgeous. And hot, very hot. After rolling off the bed, he shimmied out of his pants. His ass did not even jiggle because it was pure muscle. His legs were so strong and so cut. My mouth was watering before he even unwrapped the condom.

Sitting up, I smacked his hand away and took ahold of him. He groaned as I pulled him to me, his cock thick and throbbing in my hand.

"I usually wouldn't let anyone guide me by my cock."

I glanced up at him, a grin pulling at my lips as I brought him to my mouth. "Maybe because you haven't met someone like me?"

His eyes were wild with lust as I took him slowly between my lips, running my tongue along the tip of him and tasting his precome. His groans were loud and earnest as I took him to the back of my throat, gagging on the size of him before repeating the motion. He fisted my hair. I could see his toes curling against the carpet, the veins rising in his legs as he rocked into my mouth. When I glanced up, he looked like fucking Adonis, so beautiful and tall. A light sheen of sweat was covering his body, and every single inch of him was just stunning.

Running my tongue along the bottom of his shaft, I pulled back and looked up at him, but his eyes were closed. "Do you want me to keep going? I think you're about to come."

"I am. I do." He somehow got the words out, but then he was moving, pushing me back against the bed. "But I would rather be way deep inside you when I do," he answered, sliding the condom on before moving to the entrance of my pussy. Pushing my booted leg back, he held the weight of that leg by the back of my knee and used his elbow to hold my other leg. Then he pushed deep into me, filling me completely and utterly. My dreams could never come close to this.

That was a fact.

It was like stars went off behind my lids as I gasped out. He was so big, stretching me, but I wanted it. I needed it. And when he started to pump into me, his body slapping into mine, I was completely lost. Everything disappeared, and there was just us, our bodies, our sweat, commingling and becoming one. Opening my eyes, I watched him, his brows together, his face taut but oh so beautiful. His shoulders were tight, his muscles bulging, and I could tell he was fighting his release. I could feel it, but it was too much. Everything was too much. My body was doing its own thing, and I couldn't fight it.

I came.

Hard.

With a shout, he came too.

Falling onto me, his face mushed my breasts as my legs fell over his shoulders in what should have been the most uncomfortable way, but it was comfortable.

And I knew that was very bad.

Kissing my left boob, he wiggled his way up my body, making me laugh before he sloppily kissed the side of my mouth. "I think you killed me."

I giggled, wrapping my arms around his neck, and to my surprise, I kissed him on his nose, his cheek, and then his eyelid. I inhaled hard, his cologne tickling my senses. "I think I am dead."

"What a way to go, huh?"

"It wasn't bad."

"It sure wasn't." He exhaled hard. I felt him moving, and then I heard the snap of the condom before he pushed himself up. I watched as he tossed it in the trash can before lying back on me. "I'm not hurting you, am I?"

"Not at all," I answered as he gathered me in his arms.

"Good. I'll get up in a few."

My lips curved into the biggest grin as I pressed my lips into his hair. It smelled woodsy and manly. "I didn't take you for a cuddler."

"I'm not."

That made my grin grow more, but it also sent pure fear to my soul.

Because I wasn't either.

But there I was.

In Gus Persson's arms.

Cuddling.

CHAPTER TWENTY

BO

I wanted to say I got every bit of desire and need for Gus Persson out of my body with our one night of fun, but my pants would have one hundred percent burst into flames.

God, he was almost perfect. That mouth, that body, that, ugh, everything. I could still feel him, still smell him, and all that was so damn bad. The more I thought about it, though, the more I didn't want to be right. I didn't want to be smart about this. I wanted to be young and free. I wanted to let go and be with him with nothing holding me back.

But everything was.

Holding his phone in my hand, I twirled it around my fingers, biting into my lip. His lock screen was a picture of him with his parents. He wasn't lying when he said they were young. They looked maybe ten years older, both so youthful and so proud of him. His mom mirrored him with the dark looks and green eyes; she was gorgeous, but so was his dad. His hair was a little lighter and his eyes were a hazel color, but he was built like Gus. Big and strong. They looked like a poster family for a cover of a magazine.

But Gus, he stole the picture for me. He was wearing a

Tornadoes jersey. His face was so bright and there were tears in his eyes. Every hope and dream became a reality in those eyes. He was stunning, and I wanted to see that smile. I wanted to feel those eyes on me. Just by looking at his face, I was back in the exact place I never wanted to be again.

A girl with a crush on a guy who could promise her nothing but a little fun and no future.

As if the universe knew I was already kicking myself for repeating the same stupid mistake, my phone rang. It was my mom. I didn't want to answer it, but I did since she didn't call unless she needed something. "Hey, Mom."

"Hey, honey, what are you up to?"

"Just got up about an hour ago."

"Did you not have school today?"

"Nope, but I have two hours of internship and a game later tonight."

"Fun," she said, right as Davis yelled something in the background. "Okay, love, yes, we'll go in a second. Wanna talk to Boo?"

Davis had called me Boo since the moment he started talking. It was sweet. He must have said yes, because his voice came over the line, sounding excited as he said, "Boo, I'm playing hockey!"

"I know, bud, I heard! Do you love it?"

"I do! You have to come watch me."

"I'd love that."

"I miss you."

My heart warmed. Sometimes I wondered if he really loved me or even really knew me enough to notice I wasn't around. "I miss you, bud."

"Okay. Here is Mom."

My mom came back on the phone, and I could tell she loved our exchange, but I couldn't ignore the pangs in my heart. "I was actually calling to see if you'd be able to make it back home for a game. I emailed you the schedule. Daddy and I will pay to fly you home. We want you to come."

"Oh," I said, surprised by their offer. "Yeah, I'd love to come. I gotta look at the schedule, and maybe I can come when the Suns are gone a few days."

"That would be great. We miss you around here."

"I miss you guys too."

"Good. Let's try to make this happen. I know you're very busy."

"I am, but I want to come."

"Good. Let me know," she said just as Gus's phone went off. A new photo of his mom appeared. He had her in his phone with the contact name Coolest Mom in the World, with, of course, a lot of heart emojis. It was adorable, but I didn't dare answer. I hit the mute button, but at the ringtone, Mom asked, "What was that?"

"Oh, just Lizzy's phone."

"Ah okay. Well, honey, I'll let you go. Talk soon."

"Yeah, I'll email you."

"Great," she said. But instead of saying bye, she blew out a breath. "I'm hoping you don't let us down."

There it was.

"I don't want to."

"Good," she said, and then the line went dead. Rolling my

eyes, I threw my phone down just as Gus's started singing with a text from his mom.

Coolest Mom in the World: *I could be on my deathbed and you aren't answering, you jerk. Why the hell aren't you playing tonight?*

I grinned. My mom would never speak to me like that. With us, it was different. Too much had happened. I had let her down like she not-so-gently liked to remind me. Often. I wasn't the daughter she raised, and it bothered me that she couldn't see the good in me. I was a decent person. A little burned here and there, but I was nice. Good. I had worked so hard to put the past behind me. To make something of my education and opportunities—even if MPT wasn't Stanford. But here was literally the coolest mom in the world trash talking her son, while my mom was just hoping I wouldn't disappoint her. Again.

Disgusted with myself, I looked down at his phone, and I swear it was taunting me. I couldn't believe I actually felt jealous of Gus's relationship with his mom. I knew I shouldn't look through his phone, but I wanted to. Desperately. So I opened it. He wasn't lying—it wasn't locked. He had tons of text messages, mostly from his mom, dad, and Max. There were a few from a guy named Mike and then tons from numbers that had no names to them. They were obviously from girls he had slept with. I scanned the texts, all begging for more of the amazing Gus.

I ignored those.

I went right to his pictures. Mostly the album was just

him, his friends, his parents, and lots of him playing hockey. He wasn't joking when he said there were videos, but unlike what I assumed, they were videos of him on a lake, playing hockey and doing tricks. He was so talented. It was mind-blowing watching him play around, laughing and just being him. He seemed like such a vanilla guy, but then I noticed the folder labeled Nasty Shit. There was the mother lode of videos of girls jiggling their tits, getting themselves off, and pictures of more of the same. I couldn't help but laugh.

He was just as dirty as rumored.

Inhaling hard, I threw the phone on the bed and then fell back, exhaling the breath I'd been holding. "What the hell am I doing? I know this won't last. I am legit setting myself up for failure. Not only is he a horndog, and yeah, I know he is probably the best lay of my life, but he isn't going to stay. He is going to leave, off into the fast lane of being a rookie in the NHL. He won't have time for me." Covering my face with my hands, I groaned loudly. "I know better!"

"Okay, the talking to yourself thing is getting weird."

Peeking through my fingers, I saw Lizzy standing at my bedroom door. She was holding her shoes in her hands, and she looked like she had been ridden hard and put away wet. "Girl," I said. "You look *rough*."

She nodded. "Lots of tequila and sex will do that."

I giggled loudly as I shook my head. "Did you at least have fun?"

"I did," she said softly, toeing the carpet. "It was a great time."

"Good."

"How about you? You have fun with Mr. Persson?"

My grin must have given it away.

"I knew it."

I rolled my eyes, looking away, trying to play as if I wasn't still pulsating from the night before. "Whatever."

"I hope you didn't get attached since you won't be seeing him around anymore."

My heart sank at her words. I knew the truth, I did, but before I could tell her that he was actually coming back to get his phone, there was a knock at the door. She looked toward the sound and then back at me. "You expecting someone?"

I was, but not this early.

I got out of bed and hobbled past her. When I opened the door, I was greeted with a happy bark from the sweetest little beagle mix. And Gus. Grinning at me.

"Oh my goodness! Look at her," I said, falling to my knees to pet the pooch as she licked me happily.

"Told you, she's gorgeous."

"She is!" I grinned, and he smiled back down at me. When he bent down, he brushed my chin with his bad hand.

"I'm here early."

"You are." I stood and pulled my focus away from Sweetie to the real reason he was here. I tried not to feel my heart sink. "I'll go get your phone."

He stopped the word by pressing his lips to mine, taking away every single breath and obliterating every fear that threatened my composure. He pulled from our kiss slowly, pressing his nose against mine. "I've had the taste of you on my lips all night and day. I've been dying for more."

I inhaled hard. "Your mom called."

He shook his head. "I'll call her later. Get your shoes on. Let's go."

"Go?"

"Yeah, breakfast, since I couldn't wait for lunch."

"You couldn't?"

"I couldn't," he agreed. "So come on. I got us some really unhealthy breakfast sandwiches and some ice cold OJ. I got Sweetie some bacon."

I just looked at him. "You're serious?"

"Duh." He laughed. "Come on."

I wasn't sure what to say, so I just said, "Okay."

When I turned, Lizzy was watching us, her eyes wide. I went back to my room and calmly slid my good foot into a flip-flop. I grabbed both our phones and my purse and then headed back to the living room, where Lizzy was still staring at Gus with her mouth hanging open. He pointed at her.

"Is your roommate broken?"

I shrugged. "She's probably freaking out that you came back. Everyone knows about Gus Persson. One and done."

He waved me off, laughing. "That's for everyone else but you. Come on."

He reached for my hand, pulling me with him, but I didn't miss the way Lizzy was still gawking at us.

I was pretty sure my expression mirrored hers.

Because I sure as hell didn't believe this was happening.

CHAPTER TWENTY-ONE

GUS

I could tell Bo didn't think I'd come back. I wasn't sure why she would think that, though, especially after last night, but I could see the shock in her eyes when she opened the door. I thought the night had gone great. I thought we vibed just as well in bed as we did out of it. We were good, real damn good, so her fears of me not keeping my word were pointless. I kept my word. I wanted to see her. I needed to see her. I wasn't even thinking of my phone last night. All I thought about was her and the noises she made when I was deep inside her. Not just that, but the way she made me laugh.

I didn't expect her roommate to look at me the way she did, but then, I guess I had earned that shitty reputation around the Suns' compound.

Oh well. Things change. People change. And Bo was definitely a woman worth changing for.

Sitting across from her on the blanket, I dug my feet in the sand as Sweetie ran through the shallow ocean waves, jumping and having a blast. Bo looked like she'd just rolled out of bed. Her hair was up in a wild bun, and she wore thick black sunglasses over her eyes. She was wearing a pair of short shorts and a big Suns Ice Girl sweatshirt. It gobbled her up, and I was jealous of it.

I wanted to gobble her up.

Glancing over at me, she smiled. "Aren't you worried she'll take off?"

I shook my head. "No. She's stuck like glue to Max and me. He tried to say he's keeping her. I'm not playing with him... I saved her. She's mine."

"Exactly," she agreed, pointing a slice of bacon at me. "I'll fight him on that."

I smiled. "You'd fight someone for me?"

She rolled her eyes and leaned back on an elbow as she ate. And, of course, changed the subject. "Miss your phone last night?"

I shook my head as I looked out at Sweetie. The water was freezing, and hardly anyone was out. It was early and sort of chilly for a November day. Taking a bite of my eggs, I said, "Nah, I was busy playing with my Sweetie."

She smiled. "I looked through it."

"Of course you did." I laughed. "I expected you to."

"So you cleared it first?"

I scoffed. "No, everything on there is always on there. When did I have time to clear it? I legit pulled it out of my pocket and handed it to you."

She gave me a sideways glance, a little smile pulling at her lips. "I still can't believe you did that."

"I really wanted you."

Her smile fell off a bit as she looked down at her plate. "And now?"

I chuckled. "Oh, Bocephus, if only there was no one here and my dog didn't need my attention..."

A gorgeous flush came over her face as she grinned. "So, this isn't over?"

"What is *this*?" I asked, because I honestly didn't know. "You keep saying this, but I have no clue what that means. Like Max fucked with me last night, saying we're dating. Are we dating?"

She looked really uncomfortable. "Do you wanna date?"

I gave her a dry look. "I asked you first."

"And I asked you second, so you gotta answer!"

I shook my head. "You're annoying, but dating, um...that's basically where I don't date anyone but you, and you do the same but with me, right?"

She slowly nodded. "Yeah."

"Then yeah, I want to do that."

She seemed shocked, her brows pulling together, and that little twitch at the side of her mouth went nuts. "You do?"

"What the hell? I said it, didn't I?"

She made a face and pressed her hand to her chest. "Excuse me, I was just verifying."

"I don't say things I don't mean, I can promise you that."

Her eyes met mine, dark and unsure. "Hey, do me a favor."

I shrugged. "Kiss you, done," I said, leaning toward her, but her hand stopped me. "That wasn't it, was it?"

"No."

"Then what?"

"Promise me you'll make no promises."

I frowned, unsure what she meant. Didn't girls want the

promise of forever and all that shit?

"I don't want to get all into this when you're going off this way and I'm going the other. I'm all for having fun and being together. That's great, but I don't want to promise anything." I couldn't see her eyes through the sunglasses, but her voice sounded guarded.

Still, I couldn't deny what she said struck me. Why did this hurt? Not really a pain, but a sting. Her words stung. Like that sucked. I wasn't saying I wanted forever and all that shit, but man, maybe I wanted some of it? Shit, what did I want? What the hell was I doing? This shit wasn't even on my radar a few weeks ago, and now, I was on a blanket with a girl of, fuck, my dreams, and I was confused.

Shit. I guess this really was dating, wasn't it?

"Okay, I'm not sure what I'm agreeing to here, but cool, no promises."

"Cool," she said softly, seeming pleased by my answer.

"But what if I want to promise something?"

"Don't."

"What if it's endless amounts of my face between your legs?"

She thought that over. "Okay, that is promise-able."

"Okay, and if I want to promise endless orgasms?"

She smiled. "That's fine."

"What about lots of sex, especially from behind?"

Her face broke into a grin. "I mean, I won't complain."

"So sexual favors are a go, but promises about futures and shit like that are a no-go."

She nodded. "Exactly."

"Because you're relationship-phobic?"

She glared. "I am not, and don't act like you know what you're talking about. You just decided to date after years of rocking that solo life."

"Hey, that was by choice. No one was ever worth it."

She gave me a dry look. "How many women have you slept with? A hundred? And not one was worth it?"

"Nope," I said with a shrug. "I am very particular."

"Whatever."

"No, it's not whatever, and I'm gonna show you. It's okay to trust someone who will promise you something."

"Oh, please... Until you've been left, heartbroken, don't talk to me about trusting anyone."

Reaching out, I cupped her by the back of her neck and brought her to me. Looking deep into her eyes, I smiled before pressing our lips together, the taste of her driving me wild. She placed her hand on mine as we kissed. Pulling back, only a breath away, I whispered, "I won't do that to you."

Her eyes were sad as she whispered back, "I've been told that before."

I really did hate this dude. "I'm not him."

"I know."

"Good, so don't punish me for his shit," I reminded her.

"You're right." She nodded.

Capturing her bottom lip with my teeth, I whispered, "I want that story."

She shook her head, releasing her lip from my hold. "And I'm nowhere near ready to rehash that shit show with you."

I pressed my nose into hers. "Still, I want to know."

She kissed the side of my lips and sat back up, reaching for her orange juice. "Believe me, you don't. It's the same old sob story. Girl falls for guy, gives him every single piece of her, shit goes down, he promises her the world and then some. Next day, he's gone."

I could see the pain in her eyes, the way each word was like pulling a knife out of her back. And chest.

She looked up at me and shrugged. "I'm sure you've heard that one before."

"He sounds like a douche."

She scoffed. "I thought he was my forever." She laughed. "I was a stupid, naïve girl."

"Give me his name. I'll rip off his limbs and present them to you."

She giggled. "How romantic."

"Right?" I asked, and then I put my food down. I reached for her, pulling her by her arm. She laid her food down before scooting into my arms and leaning her head against mine. She smelled clean, like deodorant. Nothing fancy, but still, I liked it.

I liked her.

A lot.

Kissing her temple, I looked at Sweetie, jumping in the waves like a crazy dog, and exhaled hard. "I request your permission to allow me to promise you something."

She groaned beside me. "No promises, Gus."

"I'm doing it anyway," I demanded, even with her resistance. "Because I'm not going to fuck you over, Bo. If I start feeling like this isn't good, then I'll tell you."

She looked up at me, and I could see how much that meant to her. "Thank you."

"I would never intentionally hurt you. And besides, my mom would kill me if I did."

She giggled as she leaned back into me, her head on my shoulder. "I mean, let's be honest, this isn't serious or anything."

Oh. I thought it could be. "Yeah," I agreed. "Just two crazy kids having fun."

She kissed my jaw. "Exactly."

"Cool."

With a giggle, she asked, "What will all your little fans say?"

I shrugged, my face scrunching up. "Who the fuck cares?"

Her eyes widened a bit, and I realized that might have sounded a little as if this was serious, so I covered it by laughing. But then, out of nowhere, Sweetie was crashing into us, shaking water everywhere and barking happily.

But all I heard was Bo's laughter as she kissed Sweetie on the head. This woman was not the least bit worried about the water or even the sand.

And at that moment, I knew this could be serious.

I just needed Bo to realize that.

CHAPTER TWENTY-TWO

GUS

"Oh, I need a shower. I smell like dog and ocean." Bo laughed over Sweetie's barking.

I put my truck in park in front of my place. "I know. I'm sorry. I'm gonna take her in, and then we'll go back to your place."

"Don't be sorry. It's fine, but what about you?" she asked as I got out of the truck's cab. "Don't you need to shower? Want me to Uber home?"

"No way," I said, shutting the door, but she got out too, which confused me. "You can stay here. I'm gonna go get her upstairs. I'll be right out."

She pointed to my pitiful dog, still wet and full of sand. "Doesn't she need a bath? You can't leave her in your apartment like that."

"Crap, yeah," I said, and I felt frantic. I knew she had her internship tonight and then the game. We'd spent too much time at the beach, but then, I wouldn't trade that for the world.

"How are you going to wash her? Is Max home?"

Fuck. "No. Crap."

I really didn't want her to Uber home. I didn't want to

waste that time. I wanted to spend it with her since we would be leaving on a road trip in a few days, and apparently, she had a lot of schoolwork to do the next couple days.

"I'll help you shower her, and then I'll shower here, put on some old clothes of yours, and get dressed at home, if that's okay," she decided and then smacked her hands together. "Cool, let's go."

Before I could agree or disagree, she took the leash and started toward my condo. I rushed to catch up with her, and once we were inside, we got Sweetie in the bath. Thankfully, Max had gone shopping for Sweetie, and there was dog shampoo, because I wasn't sure how I felt about my baby girl smelling like Max's nasty body spray. I sure as hell wasn't using mine on her. Wasn't sure that was even safe.

Rubbing soap into her ears, Bo kissed her nose. "Aren't you a spoiled girl? Yes, you are," she cooed, kissing her again.

"Can I say I find it hot that you love dogs?"

She looked over at me and threw a handful of suds at me, hitting me right between my brows. "Stop, horndog. We don't have time for your shenanigans," she teased.

Wiping my face, I stuck my hand in the bath and glared. "Rude."

"Not rude!" she teased as she went back to washing Sweetie, but just as she went from her back, I gathered a whole fist of suds and threw them in her hair.

"Gus!"

"What?" I asked innocently. When she went to throw more at me, I held up my hand. "Bad hand! Truce!"

She paused, rolling her eyes. "Fine, truce."

Bo went back to washing, and I grinned at her as I leaned back on my haunches as she washed my dog. "You're lucky I have a bad hand."

She smiled over at me. "Oh really?"

"Oh yeah," I said, moving closer to her and nibbling on her neck. "I would throw you in this bath, get you all wet, and then fuck you against the tile."

She gasped, but I could see the grin on her face as she lifted her shoulder to push me away. "I am washing your dog. Please. You're so distracting."

I fought back my laughter as she rinsed Sweetie down. She looked like a damn hot mess, hair everywhere, her shirt and shorts soaked. Sand was scattered through her hair and had dried against her neck. Still, she was beautiful, so fucking beautiful. I wanted her.

Bad.

"Think we have time for a quickie?"

She looked over her shoulder at me. "Gus!"

"What? I'm fucking burning hot here, baby."

She sucked in a deep breath, shaking her head as she reached for the towel she had out. Without answering me, she carefully lifted Sweetie out of the bathtub and dried her. Sweetie took off like a bat out of hell, and I laughed.

"Bet you anything she's on the couch, rubbing herself all over it. She did that to Max yesterday."

When I glanced back at her, she was lifting her shirt. My mouth dropped when I realized she wasn't wearing a bra. Again. "Do you have something against bras, Ms. St. James?"

She gave me a kitten smile. "Is that a problem?"

Taking her in my arms, I held her tight so her breasts pressed against my chest. "Not even close to a problem."

As her mouth met mine, I carefully lifted her with one arm. She wrapped her good leg around my waist and kind of awkwardly held up the boot. It reminded me of the first time we got hot and heavy, which did nothing but make me harder. Her mouth was torturing me. She rubbed her tongue along my lips and swept my tongue in the most erotic way. I wasn't sure when Max would be home, so I used her ass to guide my bedroom door closed. She helped me yank off my shirt, kissing down my chest as she went. She pecked at my nipple, sending chills down my back, before she slid down my body, pulling my shorts down and taking my engorged flesh in her hand. She moved her hands up and down me and followed with her mouth. I couldn't stand how fucking great every kiss, every touch felt. This could never be just one and done. Not her.

All rational thought stopped as she swirled her tongue along the tip of me. I threw back my head, and she sank to her knees. She cupped my balls and took them in her mouth, sucking them a bit before kissing my thighs and then my hips. "Are you ready?"

"Fucking hell, I've been ready," I moaned before pulling her up by the back of her elbows and hard against me, capturing her mouth with mine. "I'm almost always ready when it comes to your sexy ass."

She bit into my lip, and I cried out softly.

"Then fuck me," she whispered.

"Don't have to ask me twice," I muttered against her mouth.

We tumbled onto the bed, careful of each other's injuries. "We are a mess."

She laughed. "We are," she agreed, kissing my wounded hand.

"I'd kiss your foot, but that's gross."

"Agreed," she laughed as she shimmied out of her shorts. I wanted to watch her, but I really needed a condom, so I opened the drawer for one. I was about to close it when she stopped me and reached in. "Unicorn Spit? What the hell?"

She held up the bottle of lube that I used to whack off, and I shrugged. "It smells good. Like donuts."

"You use this?"

I scoffed. "All the time."

"You whack off with stuff that smells like donuts."

"Yeah, and then I go eat donuts. It's actually a damn good time."

She giggled and opened the top. "Oh wow, it does smell good."

She squirted cool lube all over my cock. I jumped at the shock of the cold, but then her mouth was on me, licking and sucking the lube. "Holy fuck."

Looking up, she beamed at me. "It tastes like donuts!"

I laughed, but it fell off quickly when I was back in her mouth. Gripping her hair, I guided her down my shaft, but then she pulled her mouth from me and we kissed. She tasted so damn sweet. Pulling back, I laughed. "Damn, that does taste good."

"Right?" she asked, leaning back and opening her legs for me. I was famished at the sight of her perfect pink pussy.

She squeezed the bottle, the lube falling and mingling with her own juices. I couldn't breathe. I wanted her. "Want a taste?" she asked innocently, moving her fingers through the lube and her own arousal.

Boy, did I.

Bo lay back against the bed so I could lick her free of the lube. I wasn't going to miss a spot, and her moans and giggles turned me on even more. I gave her clit the love that I wanted to give it all the time. I took my time, drawing out each lick, suckling and lightly nipping at her hard nub. She was squirming and jerking as my name came out in spurts. Her whole body was flushed as she arched off the bed, crying out as she hit her climax. When her legs started to shake, I laughed, kissing her knees before reaching for the condom.

"Ow."

I looked up at her, and gone was her O face. Her face was scrunched up, and she was leaning to the side, drawing her legs together. "What's wrong?"

"Ow! I don't know!" she cried out, opening her legs before she started to fan her pussy. "It burns! Oh my God!"

"What burns?" I asked as she screamed frantically, squeezing her legs together.

"My pussy! Oh my God, Gus!" she cried, and for a second I thought she was joking, but then she opened her legs, looking down at it as she fanned it even more.

Looking between her legs, my eyes widened, and then I started panicking. "What the hell is wrong with your puss?"

CHAPTER TWENTY-THREE

BO

Pressing my fingers to my nose, I closed my eyes as the doctor went on.

"The swelling will go down and the hives will go away, so don't worry about that. The reason you couldn't breathe was because you had a panic attack—we think. But all in all, you're fine. Just never use, um...errr...Unicorn Spit."

I wanted to die.

"Duly noted," Gus said beside me.

Yup, I definitely wanted to die.

"Or better yet, any lubricant. I think you may have an allergy to lubricants. Are you allergic to latex?"

Someone kill me.

"No, we've used condoms, and she never did all that. I mean, you saw it. Her pu—errr, I mean, vagina... It was huge."

Oh, so it's funny to let me die slowly? Great. Thanks, universe.

"Oh, okay, then it has to be something in this lubricant." The doctor—who, by the way, was very good-looking—asked, "This was the only lubricant you've used?"

Gus, not even the least bit embarrassed, nodded. "Yeah,

she's usually good without it. We got a little freaky, if you know what I mean," he said, wiggling his brows.

"Oh my God, Gus. Shut up!"

He just laughed. The asshole laughed.

"It's really no big deal," the doctor said over a smile. "This isn't even the weirdest thing I've seen."

"Wonderful."

"Really? What was the weirdest?" Gus asked.

"Wow, are we done?" I asked, ready to go.

"Um, yes, you're released, Ms. St. James. I would suggest no sex for the next forty-eight hours or until there is no more swelling."

"No problem," I said, hopping off the exam table. "I'm sorry. I need to go. I already missed my internship, and I'm hoping I can make it to my game."

Unfortunately, the doctor shook his head. "Actually, I don't want you going to work tonight. Too much walking can irritate that area. I want you to go home and take it easy. You have a lot going on there."

"You think?" I snapped, and then I held up my hand. "I'm sorry. My vagina hurts, and I'm crabby."

"With good reason," Gus added with a shrug.

But really, what in the hell was I supposed to tell work? My vagina was broken! "Ugh..."

"Can you write her a note but leave off why?" Gus asked then, coming to my side.

God bless him.

"Oh yeah, that's no problem. Just have them call me if they need any more information. I'll never tell them what is going on, though."

Taking the note, I nodded. "Thank you, Doctor."

"See ya," Gus said to him as we followed him out. "We'll need to get a beer sometime. I need to know these stories."

The doctor laughed.

Gus wrapped his arm around me, but I wanted to shake him off. I couldn't believe this was happening. My pussy was swollen to the size of a softball. There were hives, and it was scary and big, and oh my God, I wanted to die.

Now.

Through the whole thing, though, Gus was amazing. He never made me feel disgusting or anything. He freaked out *with* me, but once I started having problems breathing, it was like a switch came on. He went into saving mode, and he got me to the hospital quickly. He never left my side. He sat with me and tried to be funny, but I was so embarrassed, I couldn't even laugh. Hell, I still hadn't looked him in the eyes yet.

Out of all the things to happen with Gus Persson, I had to have the swollen vagina.

I have shit luck.

When we got outside, Gus started humming a very popular Alicia Keys song, and I whipped my head to him, my eyes sending daggers. "You better not."

"What?" he asked innocently, but he kept on humming!

"Shut up!"

He couldn't hold in his laughter. It was sputtering, his eyes bright as he squeezed me into his chest. "But your sex was on fire!"

"I hate you," I groaned as he laughed, kissing my mouth

free of its pout.

Pulling away, still laughing, he said, "I've been waiting all night to sing that, but I was worried you'd kick me out."

"I would have," I confirmed.

"Figured so. Now get in." He shut the door and then leaned on the open window, his eyes level with mine. The air was cool, and he looked beautiful standing there. There was still sand in his hair from earlier, and his face was a little sun-kissed. It was honestly stunning looking at him, but then I looked away, still so damn embarrassed.

I mean really, my vagina had to be an asshole and swell up?

How unfair.

"So here's my plan."

I looked back over at him and scrunched up my face. The plan was to go home and hide for a couple weeks. "Plan?"

"Yeah, we're both injured, can't play tonight," he said simply, his eyes sparkling with amusement. "So, I'm thinking ice cream, noodles, some Netflix, and an ice pack for your puss."

I glared, but he beamed back at me.

"We can watch whatever you want, and I'll even hold the ice pack to your pussy. *If* you want to take your panties off, I support that. We'll stay in my room."

I crossed my arms and pouted.

He continued, "I'll even let you wear some of my comfortable clothes so we don't have to go back to your apartment and face Lizzy. Remember, ice pack, your pussy, ice cream. Damn good time, baby."

Still not answering him, I glared at the dashboard.

"And as soon as you're nice and healed, I'll suck that pussy for hours on end to make sure it's happy again."

He was smiling at me, his face so bright and full of happiness. He was annoying as fuck, but then so damn adorable. Yet, I couldn't understand what was going on between us. "Why are you being nice to me? Most guys would run at the sight of that."

"Duh, I'm not like most guys. Plus, I don't care what it looks like as long as it works."

I rolled my eyes. "Oh gee, thanks."

He reached out, cupping my face. "And attached to you." Running his thumb along my lip, he whispered, "Don't be embarrassed. I'll never tell anyone."

I realized that really was the main reason I was so embarrassed. I didn't want to be the talk of the locker room. But hearing him say that, seeing his eyes, I could tell he'd never do that to me. "You won't?"

"Never." His eyes were serious and dark as they held mine. "I wouldn't do that to you."

Holding his hand in mine, I exhaled. "Chocolate ice cream?"

"Duh, with chocolate syrup."

I smiled. "And *Friends*? Can we watch *Friends*? Or *The Office*!"

"Yes! *Office!*" He cheered and kissed my nose. When he tried to pull away, I wouldn't let him. His eyes searched mine, a smile pulling at his lips. "You okay?"

I couldn't believe what was happening. Just hours ago, I

said this was nothing but fun, but something was swirling deep in my gut, and I was pretty sure it was stupid feelings for this goofy goof who wanted nothing more than to make me feel good. I wanted to believe that this could be something, but I was the girl who had the worst luck.

Hence, the swollen vagina.

Yet, even I couldn't dwell on that as I stared into those green depths of his. "Thank you," I whispered, kissing his palm. "Really, it means a lot that you were there for me today."

His face changed. Gone was the goofy grin, replaced with a serious but equally hot quirk of his lips. "Hey, it's becoming our thing, ER visits. Wonder if they'll set aside a bed for us once a week."

"Wouldn't that be cool? Have pizza waiting?"

"And lots of ice packs, some pain meds."

"Yes, and condoms, 'cause we'll have to do it at least once there."

He cracked up as he nodded. "Oh, I'd bend you over the little desk thingy with no qualms whatsoever."

I bubbled with laughter. "Whatever. You're next, so I'll probably have to give you head."

"Oh, a BJ from my BJ, how sweet."

Rolling my eyes, I laughed. "Oh, shut it."

He shrugged. "But you'll be there, promise?"

"I told you, no promises," I reminded him, but he shook his head.

"No, I want a promise on this one."

"I will," I answered automatically without really thinking. "As long as you want me."

"I will, and I promise I'll always be there with you," he shot back, mirroring my words before kissing my nose once more. "Let's go."

"Okay."

I watched as he walked around the truck, fishing his keys out of his shorts. It wasn't him that had my heart skipping all kinds of beats in my chest.

No, it was the grin on his face.

A smile that took over my world.

Exhaling hard, I shook my head because the voice in my head said, *You are positively the biggest idiot on this planet, Bo St. James.*

But I didn't care.

I didn't hate him.

CHAPTER TWENTY-FOUR

BO

"I need your notes."

Going through the door that Lizzy was holding open for me, I pulled out my notes from our last class and handed them to her. "Did you fall asleep?"

Lizzy gave me a look. "The fact that you didn't even notice me during that class is sad, Bo. Like really, how do you zone into class like that?"

"Because I want to pass with the highest grade."

"Overachiever."

"You could be too, if you weren't out sleeping with the professor all night long."

"Um, I think that's the epitome of overachiever. I'm doing that extra for the A." She giggled beside me, her lips pursing as she shrugged. "Plus, I'll take sex with Roger over that class any day, and that's a promise."

"You're insane." I laughed as I tucked my stuff back in my bag. "What are you doing for break? Please don't tell me you're going to Mr. McMillian's office."

She gave me a dry look. I know she didn't like me calling him by his last name, but he was my professor, and it was weird

TONI ALEO

to call him by his first name.

"Yes, I'm going," she said. "He brought us lunch."

"How darling."

"It is. I really like him."

"Good," I answered with a nod. "But that leaves me lonely for lunch."

"Call your little boy toy. He'll bring you something."

"I'm not going to call him to ask him to bring me food. That's so relationship-like."

Again with the dry look. "Aren't you two in a relationship?"

I made a face. "We're dating."

"Uh-huh, which means you're in a relationship."

"Whatever." I rolled my eyes, pulling my phone out to text Gus. I had spoken with him earlier, but then I was in classes the rest of the morning. I sorta, kinda, in a way, missed him. Things were good with us, like really good, and while I was still trying to hold back being honest with myself about my feelings, it was getting harder and harder by the day.

I was about to text him when Lizzy said, "Wait... Isn't that Gus right there?"

I looked up, following where she was pointing, to in fact see Gus leaning up against his truck. My face scrunched up in confusion while he pushed off the truck, his lips curving as he came toward me. "Hey."

"Hey," I said, still not sure what he was doing there.

"I brought you lunch." He reached for me and kissed me softly on the lips before squeezing my hips.

"Guess you won't be alone now," Lizzy sang as she started off the other way. "Bye, Gus."

"See ya," he called before he wrapped his arm around my neck, pulling me close. "Are you hungry?"

I leaned my forehead into his cheek. "Starving. What made you think of doing this?"

He chuckled. "I just figured you'd be hungry since you had a long day. Plus, I just wanted to see you."

"You did?" I asked. I felt my heart flutter as we reached his truck.

"I *so* did," he answered. He reached for the bag of Panera and then guided me to the bed of the truck. "I've been thinking about you all morning."

"Whatever. You were not." I giggled as he brought the back hitch down. He took my hand and helped me up into it and then set the food beside me.

He shot me a look as he hopped up with ease. "I did too. You're all I think about."

That warmed me from the inside out. "Well, that's a nice thing to say."

"It's the truth." He handed me a salad and cup of soup. "That's what you like, right?"

I smiled as I nodded. It blew me away that he remembered what I ordered the last time we went. "It is."

"Good." He dug into a hearty sandwich and a bag of chips. "So you leave in a couple weeks?"

"Week after next." I wasn't necessarily dreading going home, but I wasn't too excited. My parents, or better yet, my mom, were a bit trying, to say the least. While I was looking forward to going back on one level, on another, after all the stuff that had gone on between us, I was dreading all the drama

I knew I'd have to face.

He nodded slowly, and I could tell he wasn't too pleased I was leaving.

"Don't want me to leave?" I asked.

He shook his head. "No, but then I'm leaving too for a couple days, so we'll both deal."

"Have you heard good things about long-distance relationships?"

He scoffed. "Relax, Bocephus. It's a road trip and a trip home for you. It's not like I'm moving. We'll be fine." I sent him a grin, and he shot one right back before he asked, "How was class?"

"Long."

"Cool. How much longer do you have in school?"

"I graduate in May."

"That's awesome. Not much longer."

"Yeah, I'm excited. I'm doing really well."

"Of course you are. You're smart as a whip."

I beamed over at him. "Okay, you don't have to suck up to me. I'll sleep with you tonight."

He laughed out loud. "That's a given. Your puss is healed, and now it's time for me to make it happy."

I shook my head, completely and utterly blown away by him. He was... Shit, he was Gus, and I absolutely adored that about him. That no-holds-barred, no-shits-given-about-anything way he had. I was feeling things I hadn't felt in a really long time. Dangerous feelings.

"How was practice?" I asked, trying to distract myself from the flush warming my face. "How's your hand?"

"Fine. I got the stitches out this morning. I'm good."

"Will you play tonight?"

"Duh, and watch out, 'cause I'm scoring all the goals for you tonight."

"For little old me?" I gushed.

"Yup, for being so amazing." He laughed.

I couldn't help it. I swooned at that.

"So I gotta be honest," he said.

I looked up from my soup. "You brought me food thinking we'd do it behind the building?"

He thought that over. "Man, why didn't I think about that? Yet, not what I need to be honest about." He chuckled softly. "So I brought you food because I wanted to talk to you about where we are on the meeting-the-parents thing."

I choked a bit on my lunch. "Um. I don't think we're anywhere near that."

He made a face of distress. "See I assumed so, but my mom is being a pain in my ass about meeting you when they come this way next month for a game."

I held his gaze. "Next month?"

"Yeah," he said shyly. "She says I talk about you too much and that I need to bring you to dinner with them."

I smiled and reached out to cup his chin. "Look at you being all vulnerable and shit."

He playfully smacked my hand away. "Just say you'll go."

I laughed. "No way. I'm sure I can get something out of this."

Gus glared. "All you'll get is a nice smack to that ass if you don't go."

"Maybe I want that nice smack?"

His lips curved as he leaned toward me, kissing the side of my mouth. "Please," he said.

"Oh my," I gushed, fanning myself. "Gus Persson begging might be the hottest thing I've ever seen."

He leaned into me. "See, and every time I look at you, I think you're the hottest thing I've ever seen."

I rolled my eyes. "Stop."

"No," he insisted, nipping at my nose. "You know they call me the Bus. Nothing can knock me down. I do the knocking down. But with you...fuck, Bo, you knock me clean on my ass."

I was breathless as I held his gaze. "You're laying it on thick."

He shot me a dry look. "Just say yes so she'll leave me alone."

I wasn't sure how I felt about it. I mean, sure, we were joking around, but these were his parents. Meeting them meant something more than I wanted it to mean. I could see he really wanted me to go. That he wanted to show me off to his parents. I swallowed hard, thinking of how to lighten the intensity of what I was feeling. "Yeah, I'll go, but I want lobster."

He scoffed. "Anything you want."

"And wine, lots of wine. Oh! And ice cream."

"I love a woman who eats well."

"Then you picked a good woman to take to dinner," I said with an exaggerated wink. "Also, I want you to say all that stuff about being the Bus again. But I want you to say it while we're doing it behind the building."

He shot me a lusty look. "Done deal."

With a grin on my face, I grabbed a fork and looked down at my salad. I realized it didn't have tomatoes. That meant Gus *remembered* I didn't like tomatoes. Breathless, I glanced over at him and beamed. "This was really sweet of you."

He shot me a small little smile that tickled my gut. "It's nothing. Just a guy bringing his girl some lunch between classes. All guys should do this."

"Your girl, huh?"

He leaned over, pressing his forehead into mine. "All mine."

That fluttering feeling filled my chest as I held his lusty gaze. His eyes were so dark and sinfully sexy. All I wanted was him to take me on the bed of this truck. But then, it was more than that. I wanted every single inch of him to touch me, and I wanted to touch him. I wanted to become one with him. I wanted to consume him.

Hell, this thing really was moving from just a good time to something more. I couldn't stop it, and I'm pretty sure Gus couldn't either. Not that he would even try. I was pretty sure he was happily driving the bus that was about to go straight through every wall I tried to put up.

And I think that's what scared me the most.

For the simple fact, I didn't want him to.

I wanted to ride passenger.

Like the damn idiot I was...

CHAPTER TWENTY-FIVE

B O

Bo: *So we're gonna be cool, right?*

Gus: *About what?*

Bo: *Don't be difficult. Tho, I know that's how you love to roll. Just to drive me insane.*

Gus: *lol I won't disagree on that, but no really, I don't know what you're talking about.*

Bo: *Sure you don't. I mean when I get there. Let's play it cool. I don't want a huge spectacle around us. You know what I mean?*

Gus: *I think what you're saying is that you want me to ignore you when you get here?*

Bo: *You do that, then I'll kick you.*

Gus: *Rude. And mixed signals. Tell me what you want, Bocephus.*

He was going to drive me into an early grave, I swore it. Rolling my eyes, I leaned back in Lizzy's truck and stared at the screen as she drove.

What did I want?

We had been inseparable the last two weeks since my allergic reaction to Unicorn Spit. When we got back to his apartment, I promptly threw that bottle in the trash. I even went and got him some regular boring stuff to replace it. He wasn't happy about it, since it didn't make him hungry after he whacked off... His words, not mine.

But things were good. He was finally able to play again, and while I still had my trusty boot, I was happy. I went to school. I coached. Gus sometimes still helped, and when we were not at work, we were together. This would be our first outing since deciding that we were exclusively dating. The concept of Gus and me dating was still weird to me. Being tainted as I was, I assumed he would already be done with me, moving on, but Gus continued to prove me wrong. He was very diligent and very thoughtful. He texted me first, every morning, and even when I didn't expect it.

It was really fucking great but also had me on edge.

I was getting used to it. Getting used to feeling good about a relationship and for the first time in maybe forever, feeling good about myself. I still felt I needed to be on high alert, that I needed to prepare myself because there was no way this would last. But the more time I spent with him, the harder that was to do. I wanted to get lost in him—fall over the edge and just be. But I could not get rid of that nagging voice that reminded me that not only was he Gus Persson, the guy with one hell of a track record of loving and leaving them, but also the same Gus the Bus Persson who had a one-way ticket to the NHL.

And where would that leave us?

It scared me. It all scared me. I knew too well and too acutely how fast something that felt so good could not just end but shatter me.

Exhaling hard, I typed back quickly.

Bo: *I don't know. Just be cool.*

Gus: *I'm always cool.*

Bo: *You know what I mean! Like just greet me but don't make a big deal about it.*

Gus: *So greet you? Don't ignore you. Don't make a big deal about it. Question.*

Bo: *Yes, and yes?*

Gus: *Is the IT you keep referring to us?*

Bo: *Yes, it is.*

Gus: *Okay, so don't make a big deal about us but greet you.*

Bo: *Are you trying to get on my nerves?*

Gus: *Yes. I love that little twitch that your nose does.*

Bo: *I hate you. See you soon.*

Gus: *I'm waiting. And you're coming home with me tonight.*

Bo: *Is that a question or a demand?*

Gus: *Demand, duh.*

My heart fluttered as I shook my head. He was maddening, but shit, he was mine. All mine, and I couldn't help but love how that made me feel. How it felt so damn right. I hated how jaded I was. How, even when I was flushing over his texts and his obvious excitement over us, I still felt I had to be on the defensive. I didn't want to end up the way Jesse left me. I didn't want to have those feelings and go through not only what he put *me* through but then my family, too. Those years will never be fully behind me. And yet there I was.

Thinking about him.

Thinking about us.

Completely infatuated with another rookie who had one foot out the damn door.

Sighing deeply, I let my phone fall to my lap.

Lizzy glanced over at me. "He's giving you a hard time?"

I couldn't hide our relationship from Lizzy, even if I tried. Gus was always at the apartment or I was with him. He wasn't one to hold back how he felt either. He was always grabbing me, kissing me, and being a total dork. "Yeah," I said. "Like always."

She giggled. "It's adorable, and I know you think you hate it, but you don't."

"Whatever."

She laughed as she tapped her hand on the steering wheel to the beat of the new Ed Sheeran song that was playing. "So you leave Friday?"

I nodded, swimming my hand through the air outside the car. It was so beautiful tonight, and I was glad we were going to a beach bar. It was the perfect night for it. "Yeah, I only planned on staying like two days, but my mom wanted me to stay till Tuesday."

"You haven't been home in a while, Bo. You have a break. Go."

I shrugged and looked out the window. "It's just hard when I go home."

Lizzy scoffed. "Well, since I know nothing about any of that, I don't know how to answer."

I smiled, still not looking at her. "There is nothing to know except that when I lost my scholarship, I really disappointed my family, and my mom loves to remind me about that."

"Shit happens."

I glanced over at her. "Not to me though. I was the smart girl who had big dreams and aspirations. I ruined all that."

"Even though I know you won't answer me, I'm gonna

ask anyway," she said before glancing over at me for a second. "What happened?"

I laughed, a harsh sound without humor. "I lost my scholarship because I was a dumbass. I really don't want to rehash it all."

Lizzy let out an annoyed sigh. "I'm going to get you drunk one night and make you tell me."

I giggled. "Duly noted."

She laughed before she reached out and squeezed my wrist. "I wouldn't judge you."

I swallowed hard. "You don't have to. I judge myself."

"Well, I think you're entirely too hard on yourself."

"I know," I agreed as we pulled into the parking lot of the Sandbox, a college bar I hadn't been to but apparently everyone else had. Gus and a few of his teammates were there, which meant most of our friends were there just to see them. The Suns' ice girls were a horny bunch, and the Suns' players were also of the very horny variety.

Getting out of the truck, I pulled my skirt down some and adjusted my lacy top. Unfortunately, I had to wear a bra with it, but it was cute enough, so I made an exception. Pulling my hair up into a messy bun, I glanced over at Lizzy. She was texting.

"Mr. McMillian?"

She shot me a dry look. She looked adorable tonight in a maxi dress. Her brown hair was down and hung straight along her shoulders. "Roger, you mean?"

"Dude, he's my teacher."

"He's mine too." She flashed me a grin. "In and out of bed."

"Dirty girl."

"You know it." She giggled as she tucked her phone into her purse. "But yes, it was him. He's going to meet us here."

"Think that's a good idea?"

She shrugged. "I don't care. I like him; he likes me. Fuck everyone who has an issue with it."

I smiled. "You amaze me."

She leaned into me. "Take a page from my book. Enjoy that guy who is completely into you. It doesn't happen often."

My smile fell. She pulled the door open and held it for me. I wanted so bad to be like her. To just jump in. But she hadn't been hurt like I had. She didn't have the disappointment of her family to carry for the rest of her life like I did. She was just a girl living her life, free enough of the past to live in the moment. I was trying to do the same but had the constant burden of trying not to make the same mistakes as before.

Stepping into the bar, I looked around for Gus and the rest of our friends.

"I think they're outside," Lizzy said from behind me before she walked in front of me. "Let's get a drink first and then head out."

I just nodded since it was ungodly loud, and I doubted she would hear me. We got some beers from the bartender and headed outside.

I was only half out the door when I heard, "Hey! It's my girlfriend, Bo St. James. Look, everyone, it's my girlfriend!"

I froze at the words. My heart jumped, and I swear I almost dropped my beer. My eyes cut to Gus's as he came toward me. Everyone outside started to laugh. Lizzy about fell over just as Gus wrapped his arms around me, kissing me hard on the lips.

I wanted to smack him.

But when he pulled back, grasping my face in his hand, his eyes burning into mine, the urge subsided.

Some.

"You said to greet you, and if I had my way, this is the way I'd do it all the time."

I was speechless as he ran his finger along my lip before pressing his nose to mine. "I also don't want any fuckers here looking at you like they can have you."

Swallowing hard, I shook my head.

I was falling way too hard for this guy.

And the problem was, I wasn't sure if he would catch me or let me bust my ass.

CHAPTER TWENTY-SIX

GUS

I loved when Bo got that look in her eye.

The one where she wasn't sure if she wanted to smack me or kiss me.

It drove me absolutely wild.

I wanted to kiss her more than I wanted to breathe.

I ran my fingers along her jawline, getting lost in her beautiful, breathtaking eyes. "You look fucking hot, Bocephus."

She rolled her eyes. "Thank you."

"I wanna take you home. Let's go."

"I just got here! I have a beer to drink!"

I shrugged. "I don't care. I got one more night with you before I leave, and when I come back, you'll be gone."

"Just for a bit."

It felt like an eternity, though. "Still, we won't be in the same place for a couple days, and that's depressing."

She smirked. "I'm sure you'll be fine."

"Nope, I'll be distressed, broken, empty! Without you!" I yelled, just for attention and to piss her off. When she twisted my nipple, I cried out, arching away from her. "That's rude."

"You're rude for hollering our business. Hush." She gave

me a flirty smile as she moved out of my arms before tangling her fingers with mine. "Come on. Let's drink and hang with our people."

I shook my head. "I don't care about them. I want to be with you."

She rolled her eyes. "So needy. Come on." She pushed through the crowd, bringing me with her. As she walked, I came up behind her, wrapping an arm around her waist. She laughed, the sound so airy and perfect as we walked as one. She smelled fantastic, something fruity and light. Her hair was a mess on top of her head with little red pieces falling along her neck. She had a bit of makeup on—not much, but enough to drive me crazy with lust. She was so beautiful, so hot, and I was glad she was all mine.

Did she know that?

Nope, my Bocephus was skittish as fuck. I had all of these feelings deep inside of me that were insane. I seriously liked everything about her. Her hair, her face, her body, her laugh, everything. These last couple weeks had been fucking awesome. If work or school didn't keep us apart, we were together. Most of the time, we lay on the couch watching Netflix. When we weren't watching TV or eating loads of bad food, we were in bed, and there, life was fucking good.

But still I worried that if I did vomit my feelings all over her, she'd freak the fuck out. She had these commitment issues that were annoying as hell, and I didn't understand them. Shouldn't I be the one with the commitment issues? Yeah, she had been hurt, and I had never really put myself out there to get hurt, but still. I wasn't that douche she was with before. I, in no way, had any intention of hurting her. I just wanted to be with her. That's all I wanted. But I felt like I was up against this wall, and I wasn't sure how to bust through it just to tell her how I felt.

That I had no intentions of falling for her when I met her. But I did.

Hard.

When we reached our group of friends, she leaned her hip into my thigh. As she drank her beer, she moved her other hand along the small of my back. Holding her waist, I looked around at all the knowing and surprised looks. Max was the only one who really knew about Bo and me. Everyone else seemed shocked. Especially the ice girls. Probably because each of them had offered me anything and everything, and I'd shot them all down. I wanted to say I knew why Bo had captured my attention, my heart, and all that, but I didn't. I wasn't sure if it was because she didn't take my shit or if it was just her. Either way, these people could fuck off. I was with her, and that was that.

"I knew that night at the Penalty Box you two were gonna hook up." I looked toward Natalie, a girl I had been with and one of Bo's friends. "It was like fireworks in that place."

"Yeah," Maci agreed. "Didn't think you two would become anything, though."

Bo looked over at her and shrugged. "Why?"

She looked uncomfortable for a moment and then smiled. "Well, you know why... Everyone knows why."

Lizzy laughed at that and then sent us a small smile. "Maybe she tamed the beast?"

I found myself laughing at that. "There is no taming the beast, ladies." I felt Bo's gaze on me. Looking down at her, I could see she didn't appreciate that comment, but surely she knew I was just joking.

Apparently not.

Moving over at bit, she scoffed. "I never claimed to tame the beast."

"I didn't say you did," I answered back, and then I pointed to Lizzy. "She did. Get mad at her."

Everyone chuckled or laughed while our gazes stayed locked. "I was just joking. Don't be upset, Bo."

Pulling her gaze from mine, she flashed Lizzy a small smile. "I'm not. I'm just teasing him."

Oh, she was such a liar.

"It's not about taming anything. We're cool, and you guys aren't surprised or shocked... You're jealous."

"Oh, she told you guys," Max joked, and laughter broke out in the group, though I didn't miss the sideways glances from some of the girls. They were jealous, and they didn't like that Bo had pointed that out.

When Bo moved out of my arms, I stopped her, holding her close. "Where you going?"

"To the bathroom," she snapped, but before I could stop her, she was already moving away.

"She's pissed," Max said.

I nodded as I glared at Lizzy. "Thanks a lot, asshole."

She shrugged. "I was joking. My bad."

"Whatever. I'll smooth it over. She can't stay mad at me."

Max laughed as he shook his head. "Man, this must be

serious if you care enough to smooth it over."

I raised my brow. This was my best friend. Surely he knew it was serious. "Duh. You knew this."

Max shrugged. "Honestly, no. I didn't."

"What?" I asked, shocked. "You see us together all the time."

"Correction, I've heard you," he said, and I laughed.

"That too."

"But I seriously thought you were just hanging out and doing it. I didn't think you cared for her more than a fuck. You've never been like that."

"'Cause no one else mattered the way she does."

Max laughed. "Yeah, that's crazy. I didn't think you had that in you."

He held my gaze for a bit, and then I shrugged. "I do."

"I can see that. I gotta tell Jessica." Pulling out his phone, he flashed me a grin. "Maybe we can double date."

I knew he was fucking with me, or trying to at least, so I just grinned back. "Let me know when."

That stunned him for a second before he laughed and texted his fiancée quickly. Smiling to myself, I took a long pull of my beer as I looked around. Bo should have been back by now. I saw her walk out of the bathroom, but instead of coming toward our group, she went out the side gate that led to the shore.

I put my beer down since I couldn't take it out to the ocean and then jogged after her. When I reached her, she had her shoes off and she hugged herself tightly as the sea breeze blew her little pieces of hair around. Taking off my hoodie, I walked up behind her, wrapping my arms around her, and held the hoodie between my hands.

"Here."

She didn't even look back behind her. She just took my Suns' hoodie and put it on. When she was situated, I wrapped my arms around her and nuzzled my nose into her neck. "Well, let me have it."

"Have what?" she asked softly, leaning her head against mine.

"My comment upset you."

She scoffed. "No, it bothered me because you made sure to let everyone know taming you would never happen, so they know you are always available—"

"But—" I tried, but she shook her head, holding her finger up.

"And then I got annoyed that I felt that way, that I got upset that you were just being you, probably joking, but I immediately got jealous. That somewhere within the last couple weeks this went from just having fun to something important to me. Something where I get upset about someone else wanting you or you wanting someone other than me."

She turned in my arms and faced me. I gazed down at her, unsure what she was about to say or do.

Swallowing hard, she said, "Gus—"

"If you're about to break up with me, save it. It's not happening."

Her brows pulled together. "What? Why?"

"'Cause I'm not letting you do it. Yeah, things have shifted, they have changed, and the thing is, if you had said that, I would have gotten pissed too. I was just fucking around, promise. And yeah, I don't care that you don't like promises, 'cause I'm a promises kind of guy, and I promise you that it's okay where this is going. Honestly."

"Gus, this can't happen."

"Well it is, so accept it."

She held my gaze, her eyes searching mine as her lips pressed together in a hard line. "So I'm not crazy? You feel it too?"

I scoffed before taking her face in my hands, wanting so desperately to be closer than we already were. "Babe, I've felt like this was something since this started. I just didn't want to tell you when you were all *let's have fun.*"

She exhaled hard. "We're in for a load of hurt. You know this, right?"

"Actually, I don't," I answered, holding her gaze. There was no light except for the moon shining down on her beautiful face.

"Gus, you are a rookie with a one-way ticket out of here. When that happens, what happens to this thing we've found ourselves in?"

I shrugged. Had I thought about that? Sure, but I didn't want to talk about it. We didn't have to worry about that yet. "Am I leaving tomorrow?"

She shot me a dry look, her brows pulling together. "No, but it's going to happen."

"And when it does, we'll cross that bridge," I said with a shrug. "Right now, I want to be with you, I want you to be with me, and I want you to be jealous 'cause I get jealous just thinking of someone even looking at you."

"You do?" she asked, her cheeks warming a bit with color. "I never thought you'd get jealous."

"Neither did I," I said simply, rubbing my thumbs along her cheeks. "But then I never thought or expected some beautiful redhead to come into my life and completely turn it upside down."

A sneaky grin pulled at her beautiful lips. "What are we going to do about us?"

"Let us be," I said softly, moving my nose along hers. "Stop worrying about shit that doesn't matter right now, and just enjoy what we have."

"We do have a lot to enjoy."

"We do," I said, a grin pulling at my lips as I slowly turned her around and pressed her ass into my groin. "Like I'm enjoying the fact you're more than likely not wearing panties tonight."

She feigned shock as I slid my hands up her skirt. "Why do you assume that?"

"'Cause you're wearing a bra," I whispered in her ear, kissing her lobe. "And you never wear both."

When I found her soft and dripping wet, I smiled against her jaw. "Just as I thought."

"Proud of yourself?"

"Not yet," I breathed against her ear as she let out a little moan once I found her clit. "But I will be when I make you scream my name on this beach."

"I won't."

"You will," I demanded in her ear, kissing it once more.

"And you're going to like it."

"I mean, I won't hate it."

I smiled.

Yup, I was falling hard for this girl.

CHAPTER TWENTY–SEVEN

GUS

I was carrying the puck and darting around the ice, looking for my teammates. They were on a line change, which was fine. I had time since the other team was changing too. We were tied at one with two minutes left against the Admirals, and I was aching for a goal. I hadn't scored all game, and I wasn't sure I'd get one before time ran out. We really needed to score now to win.

When Roberts hit the ice, I sent it up the boards to him, and he took it in as I rushed with Max to the line. Roberts shot, but it went wide, and when Chomsky got it, he shot it quick, but it went off their defenseman. He hit the ground hard. He was stung, and while it sucked, I took advantage. But when I rushed to the puck, some asshole beat me to it and zipped around me.

"Well fuck!" I yelled as I chased him down, since of course, he was on a fucking breakaway.

I was able to catch up and get in front of him, and when he went to shoot, I laid out, taking the puck to the ribs, right where my pads didn't fully cover.

Of course.

"Fuck!" I yelled out as he kept jabbing me with his stick to try to get the puck. But then he was on the ground, Chomsky on top of him, pounding him in the head. I tried to stand, but then I was knocked down. A body landed on me, and then I was being called a stupid pussy. I wasn't sure what I did wrong except play my game, but then, I wasn't the nicest guy out here. We were all trying to fight for our spot. At that moment though, I was trying to get the fucker off me as whistles were blowing and people were yelling.

Loads of fun.

When it was all said and done, both teams were down two men. Sitting next to Max, I squirted some Gatorade in my mouth and looked around as they dropped the puck in our zone. My side was killing me, but I wouldn't say anything. A bruised rib wouldn't get me down.

Max leaned over. "You're making a face."

I laughed, and it hurt. "He hit me in the ribs a few times."

"You good?" he asked, worry filling his features.

I nodded. "Fine."

Our line was called, and we went over the boards with ease. Since I was a defenseman that could score like a forward, they only threw out one forward with us. The Admirals had possession at first, but Chomsky changed that the moment he got on the ice. Unfortunately, their defense stole the puck, but when they tried to pass it up to their forwards, I broke up the pass, getting control before sending it up to Max, who was moving hard up the ice with Chomsky beside him. I rushed to catch up as they tried to make a play. Max shot, but he missed, and it went up the boards to Chomsky, who passed it back to Max. One would assume that he would have shot, but he didn't have the lane, so I set up with a clear shot in my sights. Like I knew he would, Max passed it to me, and I shot, hard—and by the grace of the good Lord above, it hit the back of the net.

Throwing my arms up in the air, I cringed hard, letting them drop just as Max and Chomsky wrapped me up in a hard hug that hurt the shit out of my side.

Houston, we may have a problem.

But I wasn't telling anyone.

◆ ◆ ◆ ◆

"I may or may not have broken a rib tonight." Looking in the mirror of the locker room, I grimaced as Bo made a face at me.

"What do you mean?"

"I got beaned with the puck," I said, looking over my wound. Everyone had already left for the hotel, but I needed a long hot shower and I didn't want to wait.

"Is there a bruise?"

I nodded before flipping the view on my FaceTime so that she could see the mirror.

Bo gasped out as she gushed, "Oh my God, Gus, that looks awful. Does it hurt when you breathe?"

I took a deep breath, cringing just as I did it. "It doesn't tickle."

"You're crazy. Go to the doctor!"

"You're not here though." I pouted.

She grinned and said, "Gus, seriously."

"Seriously nothing. I can't go to the ER without you."

"Then go to the team doctor, you idiot! Jesus! What if it

punctured your lungs or something insane?"

I made a face. "I'm fine. Maybe I'll go tomorrow."

She gave me a stern look. "Now. You haven't even left yet."

"Ugh. I don't want to."

"Stop being a baby and go."

I pouted. "Will you kiss it when you get back?"

She flashed me a grin. "That and more," she said, wiggling her brows. "Go, seriously. Please."

"Fine. I'll call you back."

"I'm getting on the plane. I'll call you when I land."

I nodded as I shot her a grin. "I miss you."

She blushed as she moved her hair out of her face. She had her ear buds in, and her hair was down in big curls over her shoulders. I loved her hair down. "I miss you too, you big dork. Go."

"I am. Damn, you're mean."

"Ha. Don't act like you're just realizing this!"

I smiled as I waved, and she did the same before the call ended. Tucking my phone into my pocket, I considered not going to the team doctor, but then I knew Bo would be pissed if she found out I didn't go. I didn't want to upset her since I did that daily with my annoying tendencies. So swallowing my pride, I headed toward where the team doctor was set up. I knew he was still working on Merriam, our goalie. It wouldn't take him long to tell me if it was broken or not, but I hoped he knew I wasn't letting this keep me from playing.

Maybe I should just let Bo get mad at me.

"Hey, Persson, come in here." I paused midstride and looked into the room Coach Rowe was set up in. "I was about to come find you."

"Me?" I asked, racing my brain for any reason that my coach would be looking for me.

"Yeah you, dumbass. Come in here."

I did as he asked, and just as I went to shut the door, he held his hand up. "That's not necessary," he said simply. "You've been called up to the Tornadoes. You'll play tomorrow night. Here is your ticket to fly out in the morning."

I just stared at him. "I'm sorry, what?"

Coach laughed. "Isn't rocket science, boy. You've been called up. One of the defensemen went down last night with a groin injury. They want you. So, you'll go."

I could only blink. I knew I wanted this. I wanted it more than I wanted my next breath, but I honestly didn't think it would happen this fast. I thought I had more time. I thought... Fuck, I needed more time.

With Bo.

"Oh. Oh, shit."

Coach smiled up at me as he held out my ticket. "I want to say I hope I get you back, but I'm pretty sure I won't."

I tried to muster up some kind of emotion. "Thank you."

"You're welcome. Good luck, and if you do come back, don't let that get you down. Plenty of guys play both teams until a spot opens up. Don't worry. I believe in you. A spot will open for you."

"Thank you," I said once more, but all I could do was think of Bo and how she had been worried about just this. Meanwhile, I was too consumed with everything that involved her. But here I was, standing with a ticket to the NHL in my hand. This was my dream, what I had wanted since I was a boy. What I had worked for. Surely we could figure something out. I couldn't lose her, but there was no way I would give up this chance. And Bo wouldn't ask me to. I know she wouldn't.

Looking back at my coach, I smiled. "I won't let you down."

"I know you won't, boy. Good luck."

Walking out of his office, I ignored the pain in my ribs, which had been taken over by the strain in my chest of not knowing what would happen with Bo. I wanted so bad to believe that we would be okay, but she had already decided we wouldn't be.

And I wasn't sure what to do with that.

Or with the pain in my ribs.

'Cause I was playing for the Tornadoes.

No matter what.

CHAPTER TWENTY-EIGHT

BO

Davis was just so full of life.

"So then, Willy knocked me down 'cause he's bigger than me, though Daddy says he isn't even five, that he's ten."

I laughed as I looked over at my dad, who was smiling wide. He looked older than I remembered him being. I hadn't been home in almost a year, and it worried me that a year of my being away had taken its toll on my father. He was gray everywhere and looked every bit his fifty-five years.

"Boo! He's taller than you!" Davis took a big bite of his eggs.

"No!" I gushed. "How in the world is he playing, then?"

"He paid the league off, Mommy said."

I giggled and glanced at where my mom was washing dishes. "Mom said that?"

"She sure did," my dad said, shaking his head. "Though, I don't disagree with her."

"You guys are insane."

"It's the truth. You'll see!"

Davis took another bite, and I wanted to scream at him to stop growing. When I was on FaceTime with my mom, he looked so small, but sitting beside him, he looked huge. His red hair was a shaggy mess, and I wanted to holler at my mom to cut it. His blue eyes were bright and full of such mischief. His nose was running, and his lips were red and chapped. He'd apparently stayed out on the pond for hours the night before, getting ready to show off for me.

He was just perfect.

"She sure will," Mom said, coming over and moving her hand through Davis's mane of hair. "Why don't you go and get dressed. And grab your bag out of Daddy's truck. We'll be taking my car to the game."

With a mouthful of eggs, he nodded before hopping up. "Okay. I'll be back. Don't go anywhere, Boo."

I shook my head. "I'll be right here."

He sent me a toothless grin and ran off. Once he was out of the kitchen, I moved my fork through my eggs before saying, "He needs a haircut, don't you think?"

"Sure does, but your mom likes it shaggy," Dad said, flipping through the paper. "I don't have it in me to argue with her."

My lips quirked as I glanced back at where my mom was washing the dishes. "I'll take him today, after the game maybe."

"It's adorable."

"It's all in his eyes, Mom."

"It isn't."

"It is. He's going to look like a girl sooner rather than later. I'll take him, I don't mind."

"I don't care if you mind or not, Bo. His hair is fine," she snapped, not looking at me.

"But it isn't," I argued. "It's annoyingly long. He's too handsome to look like a girl."

"Well, it doesn't matter because you aren't here to see it anyway."

I looked back down at my plate, shaking my head. I didn't want to fight with her. "You're right."

"We can decide if he needs a haircut, Bo Jane. We are his parents."

"Never said you weren't," I said back before exhaling hard. Pushing my plate forward, I got up to take it to the sink. "I was just offering."

"Well, thank you, but we don't need it. We're doing just fine."

"I know, Mom. I never said you weren't."

"You implied it."

"I didn't, and if I did, I apolo—"

"It's over, let it go," my dad hollered from his chair. "It doesn't matter. And Rachel, you know darn well that boy needs a haircut."

"Taylor, he doesn't."

He slammed the paper down, giving her a pointed look. "He does, and listen to me right now. I'm not doing this with you two. I will not stay in an argument for the next four days. Go get the boy's hair cut, Bocephus. And Rachel, let it be. And you wonder why she doesn't come home...or hell, why she left."

Mom glared as she stuck her hands to her hips. "And what does that mean?"

"It means you start a fight over everything with her. Yesterday, it was the way she was wearing her hair. Today, it's 'cause she offered to get Davis's haircut. I don't know if you have a thing with hair or if you're annoyed she doesn't want to be here, but either way, I don't want to hear it."

I looked away, shaking my head 'cause my mom was about to blow. "Well, excuse me for causing you so much hell, Taylor! I happen to love my kids and want to not only see them but have the best for them."

"Then please, leave her alone. She's home. Let's enjoy her being home." They stared at each other for a long time before he gave me a look. "Jeez, stop arguing with her."

"I'm sorry." I then glanced over in my mom's direction. "I wasn't trying to fight with you."

She waved me off. "It's fine."

I knew it wasn't, though. She was pissed. Hell, she had been mad at me for the last six years. Since she couldn't control me, or my fate, she was dead set on doing that for Davis. He would end up hating her for it, but maybe he would be smarter than I was.

Silence stretched through the kitchen, and the sound of Davis moving through the house was the only noise as I sat there, playing on my phone, unsure what to say or do. I was ready to go to the game, and since it was obvious that my dad was pissed at my mom for being mad at me, there was no point in talking.

It would end up an argument.

When my phone rang and a picture of Gus and me on the back of his truck appeared, I smiled and answered, "Hey, you."

I felt my parents' gazes on me as I left the kitchen and moved to the back deck where it was freezing, though I didn't care. "I tried calling you when I landed."

His voice was low. "Yeah, sorry, I fell asleep. I was dead."

"Understandable. How's your side?"

"It's a little tender, but I'm fine."

I wasn't sure if he was lying or not. He was so pigheaded and wanted so desperately to play. Before I could ask him, though, he went on. "Then this morning I had an early flight."

My brows pulled together. "An early flight? For what? I thought you guys weren't leaving until tonight for Florida?"

"Actually, I'm not with the Suns today."

"Oh?" I asked, and for some reason my pulse picked up.

"Babe, I got called up."

A billion different emotions hit me at once as I stood there looking out at the pond that Davis had been on the night before. I could imagine Gus out there, all small and cute, skating and dreaming up what he wanted to be when he got older. With my heart full, I gushed out, "Oh my God! No way!"

"Yeah, I'm here in the Twin Cities."

"Gus! That's awesome." I was so happy for him. He wanted this, had worked so hard for this, but I couldn't help thinking that this could mean the end of us. Swallowing hard, I asked, "Is it permanent?"

"No, not now at least. One of the defensemen pulled something in his groin, so they chose me to replace him. But I saw him this morning, and he seemed fine. Pretty sure I'm going back to the Suns tomorrow."

Guilt flooded me within seconds when I realized how happy it made me that he would more than likely be back. "Well, that sucks," I lied, and I covered my face in disgust. I wanted him to succeed, I wanted him to do great, so I shouldn't be this happy.

Though, I was.

I didn't want us to end yet.

"Yeah, but it is what it is. I'll go out, show them my best, and hopefully a spot for me will open."

"It will," I decided. I just hoped I would be ready to lose him.

'Cause I would.

The NHL would win over me.

As it should.

"I'm so proud of you."

I could hear the smile in his voice. "That's what my mom said, but it means more from you for some reason."

Now I was grinning. "Well goodness, Gus, don't you know how to make a girl blush."

He laughed. "Only you," he said as his voice dropped a bit. "What are your plans tonight?"

"Oh, well, I'm hanging with Davis. My mom and dad are going out tonight."

"Well, I wanted you to come to the game tonight. I got you two tickets. They'll be at will call under your name. Will you come?"

"Of course. Davis would love it."

"Great," he said, his voice rising. "But there is something else."

"Okay..."

"Remember how I asked if you would be good with meeting my parents?"

"Yeah?"

"They want to take us out to dinner after the game. Is that too late for Davis?"

I didn't even hesitate. "I'll talk to my mom, but I'm sure it isn't since it's a Saturday night."

"Okay. Would you come?"

I bit into my cheek. I wanted to say yes because I so desperately wanted to see him. I missed him, but maybe it wasn't a good idea. If he was getting called up, that meant he would be getting a spot at any time on the Tornadoes. Which meant one thing.

We'd be over.

As I thought that, though, I could hear Gus in my head.

Live in the now.

"Yeah, let me make sure it's good with my mom, and then I'll text you."

"Sounds great. Hey."

"Hey?"

"I miss you so fucking much."

My face broke into a grin as I toed the deck with my sneaker. "I miss you too."

"Good. I'll see you tonight."

"Great," I said softly as we said bye. Glancing at my phone, my stomach twisted with nervousness. I was setting myself up for failure. I just knew it, yet I couldn't stop myself. I wanted to see him play on the ice that I grew up watching the greats play on. I wanted to see him succeed. The problem was, I doubted he wanted to stay with me through it all. He'd be a hotshot rookie. All the girls would want him. It was a given, so I really needed to pull back.

Get control of this crazy, out-of-control thing that was our relationship.

Exhaling hard, I walked back into the house just as Davis was running back out. My mom's hands were at her hips, and my dad was just shaking his head. "That boy is a trip."

"What?" I asked, and my mom glanced at me for just a moment before turning back to the sink.

"He wants to score just for you."

"Aw, he's such a doll."

"He is," she said, her voice tight. "If you were home with him, you'd know that."

I bit into my lip just as my dad warned, "Rachel. Come on."

But I was over it. "Mom, why do you ask me to come home if you're just going to give me shit the entire time?"

She looked over her shoulder at me. "I'm not."

"Yes, you are! I've been here for almost a whole twenty-four hours, and you've done nothing but take little jabs at me. I'm sorry! I'm sorry I wasn't the daughter you raised. That I made a mistake, but hell, let it go! It's been almost six years!"

"You walked out on us!"

"I didn't, though! We decided on this, together, as a family. You told me I was making the right decision! I did it, and now you're torturing me for it."

"You aren't here for him."

"Because you took that right from me! I'm his sister! Remember!" I yelled, shaking my head, tears burning my eyes.

"Yeah, because you couldn't handle being a mother,"

she snapped, and I glared back at her as a silence stretched between us.

"You're right. I was nowhere near ready; you told me that daily from the moment I came home pregnant. Then I was brokenhearted. I was clinically depressed for the whole nine months I was pregnant, Mom. Who would want that kind of person as a mother? Remember how you told me that? I wanted to give him up to a good family, but you insisted that you and Dad take him. You did this. You made the decision that I wasn't good enough for him. Stop throwing that in my face. I have enough guilt as it is."

My dad looked away, and my mom just shook her head. "I want you to be more involved in his life."

"I am, Mom, as his sister who is seventeen years older than he is. I'm not his mom; you are. I am so sorry that I've disappointed you. That I'm not what you wanted, but thank God you have him. He'll be everything you wanted me to be. I believe that, but every time you throw my past in my face, you're not only hurting me, you're pushing me away. So I suggest you stop." Turning my back to her, I went to leave the room, but before I stepped out, I turned and said, "I'm taking him to the Tornadoes game tonight and then going out to dinner after. We'll be home late."

"Why don't you go before?" she asked.

I shook my head. "Because my boyfriend, who is playing tonight for the Tornadoes, wants to take us out afterward."

Dad turned, looking at me, as my mom's jaw dropped. "A boyfriend? Do you think that's a good idea? Don't you remember the last time you got involved with a hock—"

"I mean, I'm almost twenty-two, and contrary to your beliefs, Mom, I did learn from my mistakes. Gus isn't Jesse. He's a good dude, and we're having fun."

"Well, does he know about Davis?" she asked, her eyes wild with anger.

"As my brother, yes. Gus doesn't need to know anything more," I said simply. "Just the way we decided that Davis would never know."

When neither of them commented or even looked at me, I walked out of the room, nothing more than a damn disappointment to both of them. I hated how this played out. I wanted to be the daughter they used to love, but with how everything had gone down, I would never be. I would forever be the one who couldn't handle anything because of some guy.

Some rookie who broke my heart.

And now I was dating another.

But Gus wasn't Jesse.

He wasn't.

God, I hoped he wasn't.

CHAPTER TWENTY-NINE

GUS

In one hand I held the first NHL puck that I had scored with.

In the other was Bo's hand.

It was easy to say, I was one happy guy.

The game was unbelievable. It was such a rush, wearing a Tornadoes jersey with my name and number on the back. Looking up in the stands and seeing not only my mom and dad but Bo too was downright indescribable. I couldn't believe it, but it was true, and I'd had no choice but to ignore the pain in my side and play my game.

And I wasn't one to point out when I played great—well, who was I kidding? I was, and I did fucking awesome.

Was I hurting now? Hell yes, but I was masking it pretty well as Bo's little brother, Davis, talked my ear off.

"What did it feel like?"

I beamed over at him. He was like a mini Bo. Those St. James genes must be pretty strong. "I don't even know. It just felt right."

"It was so cool seeing you out there! I wanna be you," he gushed, and Bo beamed over him, messing up his hair.

"You'll get there if you work hard," she said simply, kissing his temple, and he nodded up to her, the love of a thousand worlds in his eyes.

"You know, Gus used to wake up at five, hit the ice for two hours, and then go to school," Dad said before beaming over at me. "I'd watch him and think, this kid is going somewhere."

When my mom started to cry again, I rolled my eyes. "It was one game, guys. Relax."

"It's a big deal. We're all so proud of you," Bo said beside me, leaning into me. "It's a huge achievement."

"It is," Mom agreed, reaching over and squeezing the hand that held my puck.

I should probably let it go and hold my mom's hand, but I almost couldn't believe it was mine. It was such a beautiful goal.

We were up by three and killing the Hurricanes. It was awesome. I was playing hard, but I really wanted a goal. I wanted to leave my mark. With ten minutes left in the second, there was a breakaway, and I rushed with Zordekiyi, hoping to give him some room to score. What surprised me, though, was that no one guarded me. They went after him, so he passed the puck to me and I went five hole right through the goalie's legs, scoring number four for the team.

It was fucking amazing.

The crowd.

The lights.

The goal song.

Everything. It was just insane.

I still had goose bumps just thinking about it. I wanted to go back. I wanted to play on the ice for the rest of my life, but I wasn't sure about my future. I'd find out more in the morning, and that did nothing but give me anxiety.

"I remember when you asked for hockey stuff." Mom started to blubber, and I scoffed, leaning into Bo. "I was so proud."

"Sorry. I didn't realize she'd be this emotional."

"Oh, shut it," Mom yelled at me as she looked at Bo. "He was so little back then. So adorable. He was a figure skater for a good couple years until he decided he didn't like the tight pants."

Bo smiled sweetly beside me. When she first got to the restaurant, I thought something was wrong. She seemed a little upset, but once she met my mom, she lit up. Or maybe it was my mom who lit up and Bo was feeding off her. I'm unsure, but I wanted to know. Maybe I could get her to come back to the hotel with me. That would be fun. We hadn't had hotel sex yet.

Leaning into her, I was going to whisper that in her ear, but her kid brother peered over at me. "Dude, tight pants?"

He was a funny kid. I hadn't really gotten to hang with him, but I liked him so far. It was obvious Bo loved him. That was a given. With a grin, I pointed my fork to my mom. "Hey, she made me, but don't worry, I found my calling."

"That's so cool," Davis gushed, and I smiled as my mom placed her beer down, taking over the conversation.

"And boy, did he. He worked so hard to catch up with the other boys. Even when we were getting back together, he still worked even though it was an emotional time, huh, Nate?"

Dad nodded as he held my gaze, such pride in his eyes.

"He has a work ethic that can't be denied. He gets that from you, Lauren."

She beamed at that. "You're right, he does."

"I get it from both of you." I glanced up from my food to my mom. "It was a team effort. I wasn't easy."

"He sure wasn't," she laughed as her gaze fell to Bo's. "He drove me absolutely wild, I swear it, but I'm just so damn proud," she cried, and my dad leaned over, kissing her temple, and when I glanced at Bo, she was just watching them with a look I didn't understand on her face. Almost like longing. "Bo, did you know he skipped the draft so that he could go to college and get a degree? Because he didn't want to ever be without an education? I mean, how'd I get so lucky?"

"You made him who he is. You did this," Bo said then, and I couldn't stop looking at her. She was so beautiful. "I mean, like he said, it's a team effort, and not many parents can be this proud of their child that they had a hand in every step of the way."

"That's the darn truth," my mom gushed, this time tapping Bo's hand.

A grin pulled at my lips as I watched her help Davis with his cup before looking over at my mom. "How did you do it?"

My mom looked up, wiping her eyes, a little confused, as was I. "What do you mean?" Mom asked, still drying her eyes.

"Sorry, I don't mean to pry, but Gus told me the back story, and I'm so intrigued by it. How did you raise him at such a young age, and so well? I mean, everything you've said, how he has such wonderful work ethic and how he went to school before just going in. Like, players don't do that. So how? I'm just so blown away by that. By you, I mean."

A silence fell over the table—well, except for Davis, who was playing with his peas, not paying a bit of attention to anyone. Some would think Bo was sucking up to my mom, but she wasn't. I could see it in her eyes. She was genuinely intrigued by my mom. But then, everyone should be. She did the impossible. I could have become a shit kid, but she didn't let me. She stood beside me, and she loved me enough for two people until my dad came along.

In my opinion, she was the best mom ever.

Mom cleared her throat as she shrugged. "I don't know, hun. I just did. I didn't have any choice. I had no support, no one wanting to be there for me—"

"And I've apologized for that," Dad added, and I laughed out.

"We know, Dad, no need to reiterate," I teased, and he shot me a grin that mirrored my own.

While he laughed, though, I noticed that Bo and Mom were still staring at each other—a weird look on their faces as Mom went on. "I was officially on my own. Since I felt like I wasn't enough to have anyone want to help me, I decided to be the best I could be for Gus."

"And you did," Bo said softly. "You did it."

"I did," she agreed, a grin pulling at her lips.

"I envy you. That strength, that's amazing."

"Well, thank you, but I'm pretty damn sure you aren't lacking in that department. You seem like a firecracker."

Bo looked away then, reaching for the cup that Davis was trying to get once more. As she tended to him, I glanced over at my mom to see that she was staring at Davis and Bo, this look in her eyes. Confused, I asked, "Mom, you good?"

She snapped her head up and nodded. "Of course. Just so damn proud of you."

But I felt like her eyes were telling me something completely different. I wasn't sure what she was thinking. Her eyes had a certain look in them as she ate her food silently while my dad was talking to Davis about hockey. When he paused to take a drink, my mom asked, "So, how old are you, Davis?"

Davis perked up, proudly saying, "Five! I'll be six in nine months."

"He isn't counting down or anything," Bo said softly, such tenderness in her eyes as she moved his hair out of his eyes.

"Wow, that's a huge gap between you two," Mom commented as my dad nodded.

"Yeah, good on your parents. We didn't have another one because by the time we got back together, Gus was almost eight and we were both lazy."

Mom laughed as I scoffed. "You mean you were lazy and she wasn't raising another kid," I supplied, and he shrugged.

"Or that."

Mom rolled her eyes. "We just didn't want such an age gap, and we were good with us."

I felt Bo move, and then her hand was gone as she reached for her water. When I looked over at her, she looked uncomfortable. Her face was blotchy with color, and she seemed tense.

"So you were what, like seventeen, when he was born?"

She didn't look up at my mom as she slowly nodded. "Yup.

Built-in babysitter." Reaching for a fry, she shrugged. "It works for them, I guess."

Mom bit into her lips as she slowly nodded, and a silence fell over the table once more. I wasn't sure what was going on, but something was up, and when my mom met my gaze, she slowly shook her head.

I had no clue what that meant.

Before I could ask, though, my dad started talking about hockey, and then I was lost in conversation. I didn't miss that Bo didn't talk much after that. Davis did, but Bo was pretty much silent as we finished up.

Leaning in close, I whispered, "You good?"

She turned her face so that our cheeks touched. "Just tired."

"That's not okay."

I felt her lips quirk. "Oh no?"

"No. I want you to come to my hotel."

"Oh really? For what?"

"Endless orgasms."

She slowly nodded. "I could wake up for that."

"So I'll text you the address?"

"I might show up."

"You better."

She pulled back, grinning.

I kissed her nose. "Thanks for coming tonight. It means the world to me."

She beamed, holding my jaw, but that little something that was always in her eyes when she looked at me was missing. She almost had a haunted look in her eyes. Still unsure what that meant, I decided it had to be the same thing that she had been upset about earlier when she showed up. Maybe she got into it with her parents again.

"Boo, I'm tired." Davis then yawned, and Bo kissed my lips before pushing her seat back.

"Okay, that's my cue to get this kiddo home. It was so wonderful to meet you two. Thank you for having me."

"Anytime," Dad said, hugging her tightly. "We love that you've gotten Gus to settle down."

"Ha, he's hardly settled," she joked, flashing me a grin as she hugged my mom tightly. "Thank you again."

"Of course, hun. I can't wait to see you again."

Davis said bye to my parents before giving me a high-five. "Can we play sometime?"

"Place and time, I'll be there."

That made the kid beam as Bo pressed her lips to the side of my mouth. "See you soon," she whispered against my lips, and then she was walking away. I heard my dad say something about the bathroom, but I was too busy watching Bo walk away. The leggings she wore should be illegal, and her hair was all wild and down. She looked killer but also sweet with her hand in Davis's.

"Gus."

At the sound of my mom's voice, I jumped. "Shit, Mom, you scared me." But when I turned to her, her eyes were full of concern. "What?"

"That boy is not her brother."

My brow quirked before my face scrunched up in confusion. "Huh?"

"Davis is not her brother. That's her son."

"No way."

"Yes way. They are identical, and I know a mother when I see one."

I just stared at her, but then it made sense.

It's the same old sob story. Girl falls for guy, gives him every single piece of her, shit goes down, he promises her the world and then some. Next day, he's gone.

Shit went down.

She got pregnant.

Wow.

Well fuck, why did I feel so betrayed?

CHAPTER THIRTY

B O

I was putting my night bag on my shoulder when a knock came at my door. "Yeah?"

My mom popped her head in. "Can I come in?"

"Yeah," I said as I tucked my phone in the side pocket of my bag. "I was about to leave. I'll be back in the morning."

"Where are you going?"

"I'm going to see Gus."

"Are you staying the night?"

"I am," I said simply, and when I looked back at her, I could see that she wanted to say so much, but she somehow kept it in as she folded her arms over her chest.

"Oh."

"Yeah, so Davis is in bed. He knocked out in the car. He had a lot of fun tonight."

"Okay, thank you. I'm sure he did."

"No reason to thank me," I said, waving her off. "So I'll see you in the morning? Or did you need something?"

She inhaled hard, and I could see the white of her knuckles as she looked around my room. "I just wanted to apologize for what happened earlier. I was in the wrong, and I didn't realize

I was pushing you away."

I shrugged. "Thanks."

"That's not my intention. I just want you to be in his life."

"Mom, I am. As his sister, like you wanted. I asked you, over and over again, if you thought this was a good idea, and you insisted that it was. Not the least bit worried about me or how I felt. How it hurt to see someone else raise my kid. At least if he was with another family, I wouldn't have seen it, and the guilt wouldn't eat me alive, but that wasn't how it was. That's why I had such a hard time. That's why I battled depression, and that's why I left as soon as I turned eighteen."

She swallowed hard. We hadn't ever discussed this. I just always held it in. Looking away, she tangled her fingers together. "Then I'm sorry. I didn't want anyone else raising my grandbaby."

"And now, I feel the same. I'm so thankful he's here, but Mom, you gotta give me a bit of a break. It's a done deal. You're Mom, I'm not."

"You're right."

I slowly nodded. "Okay, then," I said softly. "I'm gonna go."

But I didn't move. Her gaze was holding mine as she whispered, "I do love you, Bo."

"I love you too, Mom," I said as we embraced, but I knew there would always be this wedge between us. I wasn't naïve; I knew what had happened all those years ago had ruined us. That was fine. If anything, I had grown from it, and I wouldn't find myself in that situation ever again.

But then...wasn't I?

I wasn't pregnant, thank God, but I was involved with

someone who had a one-way ticket out of my life. Someone I was falling for, hard, and that alone should have had me running for the hills.

But instead I was going to the hotel to see him.

Maybe my mom had a reason to worry...

Maybe I hadn't learned a damn thing from my past.

When the door opened, Gus had no shirt on. His beautiful, defined body stared back at me, and within seconds I was famished. I reached for him and he for me, and he took me in his arms as our mouths crashed together. I ran my fingers along his shoulders as he kicked the door shut. Pressing me into it, he moved his hands along my hips, up to the small of my back, before lifting my shirt up and over my body. Tearing his mouth from mine, he ran it down my neck to my breast, where he took my nipple in his mouth.

"Gus," I cried out as his hands moved along my body, pulling at my leggings until they were creeping down my hips. Following them with his mouth, he kissed me everywhere until he found my hot center. Moving my fingers through his hair, I arched off the door against his mouth as I cried out. I swear, he had the best mouth I had ever experienced in my life.

Opening me up, he slid his tongue up me, lapping my wetness before dipping the tip of his tongue inside me, causing my legs to shake. Holding them still, he dragged his tongue up my pussy, finding my clit before ruthlessly flicking his tongue against it with nothing holding him back.

Thrashing against the door, I cried out, his name falling

from my lips in a lusty way that urged him to go faster. When he sucked my clit into his mouth, I almost came undone. I was right there, but then he stopped abruptly before lapping at my clit. So slow and almost like torture. Barely licking me but licking me just enough to have my toes curling against the hotel carpet as I bit into my lip. Taking ahold of his head, I pressed myself into his mouth, and he chuckled against me.

"Want it, huh?"

"So bad," I gasped out.

"Say no more."

Digging his fingers into my ass, he buried his mouth in me, sucking my clit so hard, I came undone like never before in my life. Crying out, I balked against him as my legs went weak.

"Holy shit," I breathed, and he chuckled against my dripping wet center.

"Man, you came hard."

"Ugh, yeah," I gasped while he kissed up my stomach. "It's been a few days."

"Which means I'm going to get even more of those lusty little moans," he said, meeting his mouth to mine, my release all over his sexy mouth. He reached his hands behind my legs and gripped my thighs as though he was going to lift me, but he didn't. Instead, I felt him cringe against my lips.

Opening my eyes, I shot him a narrow look. "Are you still hurting?"

He shook his head. "Just a bit. I'm fine. Come here," he said, trying to kiss me once more, but I stopped him.

"Wait. Did you go?"

Tearing his mouth from my neck, he murmured, "Huh?"

"To the doctor. Did you go?"

He paused, his eyes searching mine, and I knew he was about to try to lie to me. "I was going—"

"Gus! You could be really hurt."

"But on my way, Coach called me in and told me I was being sent up. I couldn't go then."

"Why?"

"'Cause what if they would have held me back!"

"It doesn't matter if you can't play at all!"

"It's just a damn bruise. I'm fine."

I shook my head. "You need to go."

"I'm fine."

"Gus, seriously," I reiterated. "I would hate for you to be out because you hurt yourself more," I said before moving out of his arms so I could see his ribs. They were black and blue. When I ran my fingers over them, he cringed as he tried to move away. "Does it still hurt when you breathe?"

"Just a little. Really, I'm fine, baby. Come here. Let me take you to bed."

"No," I said, pushing him away as I went to touch a little more. I didn't feel anything poking, so that was good, but still he needed to go. "You told me you'd go."

"I know, but then they called me up, and I didn't want to risk not going," he explained once more.

I could see how much it meant to him. Didn't he understand that this could go bad?

"You'll go save a dog with no worries about your career, but when you really hurt yourself, you won't go to the ER to make sure you're okay?"

"I'm fine!"

"You're not, Gus, Jesus!" I yelled back, and then I glared at him, reaching for my shirt. "I can't believe you lied to me."

"Oh, come on, relax. It's not like I lied about who I was with last night. I don't even think I really lied!"

"But you did, when you promised you'd never! See, this is why I don't do promises!"

"Babe, really? I've not lied to you or held anything from you, like you're doing with me. Yet, I'm not coming at you funky. So relax."

I paused, my heart picking up in speed. "Huh?"

"I didn't intentionally lie. I was excited and didn't want to ruin my good news with the shitty *I didn't go to the doctor* news, but you've been lying to me since the moment we got started."

I put my hands on my hips and stood there buck naked and confused. "What the hell are you talking about?"

He held my gaze for a long time. It seemed that he was trying to figure out what to say, which wasn't like him. He normally just spoke and cared about the ramifications later. When he moved toward me, his eyes dark, I held my breath. "Is Davis your brother or your kid?"

All the air rushed from my body as my gaze stayed locked with his.

Oh. Shit.

CHAPTER THIRTY-ONE

GUS

Bo had such a blank look on her face.

Her jaw was hanging open, and she looked as if I had hit her. Instantly I felt like shit. I didn't want to hurt her. I didn't care that he was her kid. It didn't matter, but at the same time, it would have been nice if she had shared that information with me. I didn't want my mom telling me shit I didn't know. Bo should trust me enough to tell me that. I wasn't just some guy off the street.

I was the guy in love with her.

"Listen—"

She cut me off, though, throwing her shirt on as she yelled, "What? Why would you ask that?"

Why was she getting pissy with me? "My mom suspected it, and then I put two and two together," I answered softly as she slid on her pants. "Is it true?"

She looked up at me, her eyes wild as she shrugged, and she didn't have to answer. It was true. I could see it in her eyes, and I couldn't understand why she wouldn't tell me. "Why does it matter?"

"Because it does."

"Why? We're just fucking around, aren't we?"

My gaze narrowed. "So instead of answering me and being honest, you're going to start a fight with me?"

"You started the fight with me. You accused me of lying, when really, you're the liar."

I shook my head. "That's not how it happened. I didn't lie, I held back informa—"

"Fine, I held back information that doesn't matter! Nothing about Davis has anything to do with us."

"But it does, because if we're going to be something, shouldn't I know something like that? That's a big part of your life that I assume goes with the shit with that guy you used to date."

She was still gawking at me, her eyes wide. "Gus, we aren't going to be anything, don't you see that? You're on the fast track to the top, and I'm just trying to get through college. Stop making this something it's not."

Her words were like knives. Holding her gaze, I shook my head. "That's not true, and you know it."

"So, you aren't going into the NHL here in the Twin Cities while I'm in Malibu?" She held her hand up. "Given you don't get held back because of your injury."

I shot her a narrow look. "We can work that out, but if we can't be honest with each other, then why are we trying?"

"I never asked you to be honest with me."

"You didn't have to, Bo. I want to be. Because I want to be yours like you are mine."

Her lips parted, her eyes flooding with tears. Her lip started to wobble as she threw her hands up. "I didn't sign up for that."

"Do you think I did? I wanted to fuck you, and now I'm fucking in love with you!"

Her tears spilled over as she gazed at me, her chest rising and falling in a dramatic fashion. Clearing her throat, she looked away.

"Everything that is happening with my career can't hold us back if we don't allow it. Tell me what happened!"

She threw her hands up as she shook her head. "But, Gus, you know what happened. It's your mom's story without the damn happy ending." Tears spilled over her eyes as she looked up at the wall, inhaling hard.

"So Davis is yours?"

She slowly shook her head. "No. I mean...yes. I had him. I was pregnant with him, but my mom and dad adopted him." She wouldn't look at me as she sat down on the bed, moving her fingers together as she inhaled hard and let it out in a whoosh. "I loved him, Gus. God, I loved him. Jesse, like you wouldn't believe. We grew up together, our families were friends, and I had always had a thing for him. When I hit high school, we started dating. He was older than me by two years, and my parents were okay with it because we knew his family."

For some reason, dread filled my gut. Even knowing the end of this story, I hurt for the girl she used to be. "We dated for three years, and it was fun, hot, and silly. We were young, we were crazy, and he promised me the world. He was projected to go right into the draft, and he did. The day we found out he drafted third was the day I found out I was pregnant." She swallowed hard as she wiped her face, hard, pulling her features as she sobbed. "I told him, and he told me we were good, that he was going to make tons of money. I went to sleep with all the confidence in the world." She paused, inhaling hard before looking up at me. "He got in his car and left that following morning. When I realized it, I texted him asking what happened, and he texted me that the baby wasn't his. That I wouldn't ruin his career. He left me. He picked his career over me and his child, and that devastated me."

I sat down beside her, reaching for her hands, though she wouldn't let me. "Bo, he was a jackass."

"I trusted him. I loved him, and he broke me."

"I understand, but he wasn't a good guy, obviously."

"But I thought he was everything."

"Well, you were wrong—or better yet, he made you wrong 'cause he was a fucking dickhead."

She wasn't listening to me though. She held her face in her hands as she explained even more. "I went into a really bad state of depression. I couldn't function, which is why I wanted to give Davis up. I wasn't like your mom. I wasn't strong like she was, because everyone was against me. I was completely alone, and I lost my scholarship because I couldn't keep up with my studies to keep my four-point GPA. I lost everything, and then I had to watch my mom raise my child because I couldn't do it."

I couldn't take it anymore. I reached for her, wrapping my arms around her and kissing her temple. "Bo, it's okay. You did what was best, not only for Davis but for yourself."

"Gus, you don't understand. I'm making the same mistake."

Those words hit me as though she threw cold water on

me. I pulled back, watching as she shook her head. As I stared at her profile, my throat closed up, and she went on. "I'm falling fast for you, just like I did with Jesse, and I know I shouldn't make you pay for his mistakes, but can't you understand, after everything I've said, it's hard not to. I mean, look at me. I'm a mess just thinking about what could happen again."

"I would never do that to you," I insisted. "That would never happen between us. I couldn't do that to you. Ever." Reaching for her hands, I laced our fingers together. "Bo, I get it. You don't like promises because you think they can't be kept, but he was a piece of shit. My word is my everything, and I wouldn't do anything to hurt you. Can't you see that?"

"I want to, but Gus, you're going into the NHL. This is your dream. Do you really want a long-distance relationship holding you down?"

I just blinked at her. How could she be so dense! "Yes! I want you. Bo, I love you."

Her eyes widened as she gawked at me. Falling to the ground between her legs, I cringed a bit from the pain in my side before I wrapped my arms around her middle, holding her gaze. "Baby, I love you and yeah, that's insane because I've never loved anyone in my life except my parents, but it's the truth. I do, I love you, and I want you. I want all of you. If it's long distance, awesome. If it's you moving here with me and Sweetie, fucking great. You can be closer to Davis. I want to get to know the dude, but not only that. I want you. All of you."

"Gus—"

"Let me finish," I said, squeezing her. "I don't know what's going to happen, Bo. I could get called up or I couldn't. I don't know. But I do know I don't want to do anything if you're not by my side."

Her eyes started to mist with tears once more. "Oh, Gus..."

"You can't let the past win. It will eat you alive. We have to stay in the now, look at the future that is promising and beautiful for us." When she started to shake her head, her tears falling in heaps, everything inside me went still. "Listen, I know you don't want promises. I get it. I do, and usually, I don't make them if I can't keep them. But with you, I know I can keep them. I promise, Bocephus Jane St. James—man, you'd think by now I would be used to the length of your name," I joked, but she didn't even smile. Her eyes were full of tears; her chest was rising and falling as she stared back at me. I didn't miss the fact that she hadn't told me she loved me too. But even with that, I couldn't stop myself from going on. "I promise, Bo, I promise I'll love you, and I won't ever make you question that. I will stand by the fact that if things go south, I'll tell you, but with the respect you deserve. Though, I feel that will never happen because we're good. Bo, can't you see how good we are?"

"But—"

"No but," I demanded, shaking my head. "Can you really sit there and not know this is good? I mean, what do you want?"

She hiccupped a sob. "I want to be with you."

"Then what's holding you back? The past? This Jesse fucker?"

She slowly nodded.

"I can't fix that, Bo. It's either you want me and us, or you let him hold you back. Aren't you fucking tired of having that on you? Don't you just want to be happy?"

When she didn't answer, I fell back on my haunches, watching her. She was fighting with herself, I could see that, and it was honestly slaughtering me. I wanted so bad for her to realize what we had, but I worried that wouldn't happen. She was too hurt.

When she stood, wobbling a bit on her boot, she looked away as she moved around me. I closed my eyes, and my heart felt like it was annihilated by a million hockey sticks as I listened to her move around the room, gathering her things.

"So that's that?" When she looked over her shoulder at me and I saw the tears falling down her face, I felt my own start to fall. "You have nothing to say?"

She swallowed hard, and with a trembling lip, she whispered, "I have so much to say, but I don't know how."

"Can you not try?"

She slowly shook her head. "No, because you deserve someone who actually has her shit together and isn't caught up in the past."

And with that, she walked out the door, shutting it behind her.

Which left me, for once, to worry about my future.

Because Bo might not be in it.

CHAPTER THIRTY-TWO

GUS

"Well...well, hell, that sucks. Do you want me to come over and run my fingers through your hair like I did when you were a baby?"

"No, Mom. I'm twenty-two years old. You can't do that."

"Who the hell says?"

I scoffed as I cuddled with my pillow, holding my phone to my ear. It had been thirteen hours since Bo had left. I had slept some but not much, since I kept trying to call and text her. She wasn't answering me though. At one point I thought she may have shut her phone off. I don't know, but I did know I was hurting. The pain from my side was nothing compared to the pain in my chest.

Fuck, this did suck.

"This is why I don't mess with girls."

My mom chuckled a bit. "Oh, you messed just fine. You just didn't get close enough to get hurt."

"Yeah, that," I answered, and she clicked her tongue.

"You didn't want to feel what I felt with your dad."

I opened my eyes, my brows coming in.

"I always knew that was what it was. That's why I've never

pushed you on settling down. You'd find the one."

I cleared my throat. "I didn't realize that's what I was doing."

"Well, of course not, because for you it was normal to be wary of relationships, but Bo came in like a wrecking ball."

My lips curved as I nodded, even though she couldn't see me. "She sure did."

"I know, honey, and if it's meant to be, it will work out. She's just embarrassed right now. She's scared, and I mean shit, I couldn't imagine what she went through. Yeah, I went through almost the same thing, but then, I didn't. I wasn't in love with your dad. I didn't care one way or another if he wanted me. She did."

"Don't spare my feelings," Dad called, and my mom scoffed.

"Don't act surprised. You know the truth."

I wasn't listening to them though. I couldn't get the image of Bo sitting on my bed and crying from her soul. She was sobbing, her whole body shaking, and I had never seen her like that. She was always so hardheaded, so strong, and the kind of person who didn't take shit from anyone. Especially me. She always put me in my place. But then, over the weeks, that started to change. She started to smile more, and I thought we were good.

We were solid.

But she walked out.

She left me.

And now I was the one fighting back the tears.

"It's hard when you want someone so bad and they won't

have you. Ask your father. He knows."

I chuckled as I shook my head. "But you two were meant for each other."

She scoffed. "Please, the only thing I thought that man was put on this earth for was to give me you. After that, he was slime."

"I'm right here, Lauren."

My face broke into a grin as my mom went on. "Well, obviously that's changed. I love you, duh."

Dad said something, but I couldn't hear it because my mom was giggling into the phone. "Ew, please, I don't want to hear this."

Her laughter subsided. "Fine, sorry."

Pinching my nose, I glanced at the clock, seeing that I had about thirty minutes before I had to be at the Tornadoes' compound. "So what do I do, Mom? Do I go see her? I can find her parents' address, I think."

"No, give her space. She'll come around."

I didn't like that answer. I wanted to run to her house, beg her to see me, but what if she wouldn't come out? That would be awful, so maybe my mom was right. I missed her so much though. I wanted to hold her, tell her that her past didn't matter, that it was about what we did now. I wanted to hear her say she loved me, because damn it, I knew she did. I just knew it.

"Want me to call her?"

I made a face as I sat up. "Hell no. I'm not having my mommy call my girlfriend to make her talk to me."

"I mean, we did connect, Gus. She loves me."

That was true, but I couldn't have my mom do this for me. Plus, I didn't want her to come talk to me because my mom asked her to. I wanted her to come to me, to be with me, because she wanted me. Because she trusted that I would never in my life hurt her.

Inhaling hard, I stood up, slipping my feet into my slides since the car the Tornadoes had sent would be here soon. "You are completely right, Mom, but I gotta do this on my own."

"Oh. My baby is growing up."

I laughed. "Only took twenty-two years, huh?"

"Hey, better late than never. Dad was twenty-four when he decided to be a man."

"Laur! What the hell?"

"What? He knows this! It isn't a secret!"

I rolled my eyes, reaching for my wallet and then looking for my phone until I realized I was on it. I may be a man according to my mom, but sometimes, I wondered about myself.

"I'm proud of you, Gus, with everything. Really. You're blowing me away, kid."

I smiled, my heart warming. It felt good to have my mom say that, and I knew she meant it, but I couldn't exactly enjoy it the way I should when I wanted so desperately to just hear Bo's voice. I wanted to feel her skin under my palms, and damn it, I wanted to kiss her pouty little mouth.

"It's all because of you, Mom."

"I know," she answered simply. "Too bad Dad didn't come in until I was already done molding you into the man you are now."

When my dad hollered something, I just laughed, loving that no matter what, I knew my family would make me laugh and also have my back. "But don't worry, honey, she'll come around. She adores you. Even Dad said the same thing, that she was completely into you."

I swallowed hard. "I love her."

"I know," Mom said almost instantly. "And in my experience, true love always wins."

"That's the nicest thing you've said to me today," I heard my dad say, and my mom laughed.

"Please, I asked if you wanted to bang an hour ago!"

"And I'm out."

Mom laughed. "Love you, honey. Good luck. Call me when you find out either way."

"I will. Love you too."

After hanging up the phone, I tucked it in my pocket before letting my head fall back, looking at the ceiling. *True love always wins.* Sounded like some kind of Disney shit, but still it gave me some hope. Even though Bo was my first love and my first girlfriend, I knew that she would be my only. Since I really didn't want to die alone, I needed her to get it together and realize that I was everything she needed.

Because she was everything I needed.

♦ ♦ ♦ ♦

When I entered Coach Tribbiani's office, he was sitting at his desk with a large hero sandwich in front of him while the general manager of the Tornadoes leaned against the windows on his phone. GM Alex Haynes was a small man but extremely smart. He was the main reason the Tornadoes were actually doing something this year. He was bringing in great talent, and Coach Tribbiani was turning them into a team.

Coach was a big man. He was not only large, but his personality filled a room. He was very animated and overused the word fuck. I mean, I loved the word. I used it a lot, but even I thought he used it too much.

"Have a fucking seat, Persson."

Haynes shot me a curt smile as I sat down, and something inside me told me that I wouldn't be staying. Neither of them was smiling, and they didn't look very pleased at that moment. Maybe I hadn't done as well as I thought I had last night. Maybe I should have listened to Bo and gone to the doctor.

Shit.

"Fuck. Who's talking? Me or you?" Coach asked, and Haynes shrugged.

"Doesn't matter," he said simply, and then they both looked at me.

I was a big dude. I usually carried myself as one, but at that moment, my heart was in my throat and I felt so damn small. On the one hand, I wanted to be sent back down. I wanted to work things out with Bo, and it would be easier if I were in the same place she was in. But then, I wanted more than anything to be a Tornado.

"I can go, if you'd like," said Haynes.

"Ah, fuck off, I'll do it," Coach said, throwing his sandwich down and then setting me with a look. "All right, kid, it's fuckin' simple. Sykies is out for the immediate future. He fucking tore something instead of the pull we originally fucking thought, so

243

you're in."

My mouth parted a bit as I stared back at him. I was convinced I was being sent back down. I really didn't think I would stay, even though that was all I wanted. "Really?"

"Yup. You're a fucking beast, kid. I'm pretty pissed at this dude for not bringing you up sooner," Coach said, nodding his head toward the GM. "We fucking need you. Are you ready?"

Was I?

I wanted to be.

I was.

Fucking hell, all I could do was think of Bo.

Maybe I should tell them about my injury, get sent back down, and fix things. But then, I was okay. It hurt, but I was still able to perform. I wanted this. I needed this.

But Bo.

"I think I bruised my ribs."

Haynes perked up as he glanced over at me. "When?"

"Back when I was with the Suns."

"And you played last night with bruised ribs?" Haynes asked.

I nodded. "Yes, sir."

He looked at Coach just as Coach glanced at him. When they both looked at me, Coach said, "Well if that's how you fucking play hurt, then I'm chomping at the fucking bit to see how you do when you aren't aching."

They both started to laugh, and I joined in, though it wasn't real. Did I really just try to ruin my chances in the NHL to be with Bo back in Malibu? Was I an idiot? I must have been, because I didn't regret it, though it didn't matter. They still wanted me. I should have been proud of that.

But I wasn't.

"Well, go on and see the fucking team doctors. They'll fix you the fuck up."

I nodded as I stood. They did the same before we all shook hands. Walking out, I went the way they directed, but it wasn't like I was really paying attention. My thoughts were with Bo and how everything I had with her was probably over. I wouldn't be there to be in her face. She was leaving tomorrow to go back to Malibu, and I wasn't sure when I would be able to go back to get my stuff. Or if I even would.

When I reached the doctor's office, there was someone already in there. Leaning against the wall after being told to wait, I twirled my phone in my hand.

I either had to give up on her or on my career.

I didn't want to do either though.

And there was only one person I wanted to talk to about it.

CHAPTER THIRTY-THREE

BO

"I love this movie."

I glanced over at Davis as he was stuffing popcorn in his mouth along with candy corn he had left over from Halloween. We were watching *The Nightmare Before Christmas*. I wasn't even watching. How could I, when I couldn't get Gus out of my head? The way he looked at me when I left his hotel the night before... I felt a lot, but most of all, I felt miserable.

I missed him. God, I missed him. Yet, that didn't stop me from ignoring his texts or his calls. I couldn't talk to him yet. I was so embarrassed by my breakdown, how I basically word vomited all over him and then decided I couldn't let the shit with Jesse go. Which was just stupid. I was over him. Not only had I not seen him in years, but I didn't even think of him. I didn't even think of him when I looked at Davis.

When I looked at Davis, I only felt love. That was it. I still had some guilt from not being the woman he needed as a mother, but mostly, I just loved the kid. He was way better off with my mom. I knew that, and the only reason I regretted him being with her was that she kept on throwing it in my face. But that wasn't holding me back from being with Gus.

I was holding me back.

Scooting toward me, Davis rested his head against my arm, and I smiled, touching my head to his. Inhaling hard, I wondered what Gus was doing. I remembered him saying he had a meeting this morning. Glancing at the clock, I realized he was probably there now. Swallowing hard, I prayed that he got his spot. He deserved it. He worked so damn hard, and hell, he was playing with busted ribs and still was killing it. I had never seen someone play the way he did. He was destined for big things.

I just wasn't sure if I would be with him through them all.

I could be, if I would stop being so pathetic and dwelling on the past, but I was so scared. If I fell, if I gave in to the feelings that wanted to suffocate me, I would be his completely. But the last time that happened—well, we know what happened.

"Boo."

With a sigh, I whispered, "Yeah, babe?"

"Can you come home more? I miss you."

My heart warmed as I cuddled closer to him. "I miss you too, honey, and don't worry. I'm almost done with school, and then maybe I can move back here."

He looked up at me. "Really?"

I smiled, though I know it didn't reach my eyes. "Maybe. We'll see."

"Will you bring Gus with you? I like that guy."

My heart skipped a beat as Davis's little blue eyes gazed into mine. "Maybe, bud. Okay?"

He slowly nodded, not looking convinced as he leaned into me, his attention moving to the TV. Leaning against him, I closed my eyes as the tears started to gather in my eyes. I hated not knowing my future. Why couldn't I just have a plan printed for me that told me everything that would happen so I could make the right choice? Would I be with Gus for the rest of my existence? Would I move back home so I could be closer to Davis? But most of all, would I be happy?

I just wanted to be happy.

And the thing was, I was happy with Gus.

When the credits started on the film, I opened my eyes to see that Davis had fallen asleep, popcorn hanging from his lips. With a smile, I wiped them away and put the kernels back in the bowl, holding back my laughter. He was so damn cute. I really wanted to be home more, but it was hard. I loved my parents, but my mom made it really hard to be around them. I wasn't sure if her apology was genuine, but I guess we'd see. Either way, I would always love Davis.

As I moved my fingers through his hair, I wondered what it would have been like if I had been like Lauren Persson, raising him on my own and being the mother he deserved. As much as I wanted to believe I could have done it, I really didn't think I could have. I was in such a bad spot. The depression and Jesse's betrayal had messed me up so bad. Thankfully, though, Davis had my parents. Being able to see him like I did, hold him and cuddle him... Most birth mothers didn't get that.

But I did.

But even the joy of having that couldn't keep my thoughts. No, they kept drifting back to Gus. Rolling to my back from my side, I reached for my phone. Opening it, the first thing I saw was us making kissy faces at the camera. This guy who

I thought was nothing but a spoiled, goofy, cocky prick was actually the guy who stole my heart. I almost couldn't believe it, but I knew it to be true.

Gus was special.

Moving to the messages, I opened his text thread, reading the many messages from him asking me to text him back, to call him, but then I noticed a text bubble that indicated he was typing something. It could be a mistake, but what if it wasn't? Was he texting me right then? Shouldn't he be in the meeting?

"Isn't he beautiful?"

I jerked my head up to see my mom standing in the doorway. She was wearing a long housedress, her strawberry hair up in a bun on top of her head. Sundays were always lazy days in the St. James house. No one ever got out of their PJs.

Dropping my phone to my lap, I nodded. "He is."

She came into my room, sitting on the chair by the door, watching me. "It's been really nice having you home."

I swallowed hard, looking down at my phone to see that Gus was still typing. Deciding a text wasn't really coming, I put my phone to sleep. "It has been. I've had a lot of fun."

She gave me a look. "Have you?"

I looked away, shrugging my shoulders. "I did when I wasn't being attacked by you." I looked up, and she was watching me. "I'm trying so hard to live in the now, but it's hard, especially when my past keeps being thrown at me."

She slowly nodded, and I noticed that her eyes were getting misty, which was surprising. My mom wasn't a crier. "I think I thought when you got older you'd want him back."

I made a face. "Mom, I can't do that to him. That's unfair.

You're what he knows."

A tear slowly rolled down her face as she nodded. "I know, and I can't believe I was hopeful for that. I think I just wanted you to realize what you had done."

"I know what I did," I snapped back. "For one, I can't forget. I wouldn't forget, but I don't regret it. He is so much better off."

"I know," she answered with a nod as she wiped her face. "I just, I just worry for you." She looked up, holding my gaze. "I feel like you're moving through life with everything that happened chained to you, and you're dragging it all with you."

I blinked. "I am," I said simply, shaking my head. "I can't let it go, and when I think I am, something comes up and I reattach the chains."

Swallowing hard, she slowly nodded as more tears fell. "Is that why you came home and cried all night?"

My jaw dropped a bit as I looked down, closing my eyes. "I didn't realize you heard me."

"Daddy and Davis didn't, but I did."

Biting into my lip, I squeezed my eyes shut.

She asked, "He's the first guy you've been with since Jesse, right?"

I nodded. "Yeah."

"He must be special."

I quirked my lips a little. "He's a pain in my ass."

When she laughed quietly, I looked up and she smiled. "The best love is."

My chest seized up as I watched her while she watched me.

"Do you want to tell me what happened?"

No. Not even kind of, but she was trying. She hadn't tried in years. Swallowing back the emotion that was trying to suffocate me, I glanced down at my lap. "He figured out things about him," I said, moving my head toward Davis. "And I blew up at him, told him that I was worried he would do what Jesse did, and I walked out."

"Do you really believe he would do that?"

I looked up. She was leaning on her lap, holding her face in her hands.

"You told me earlier he was different."

"He is." I licked my lips, fighting back my tears. "He is amazing, he is funny, and he's so giving. He would do anything for me. But I know he'll choose his career over me, when he should—he's talented as hell. But, like Jesse, he loves the attention of ladies—"

"Stop right there," she said, and I looked up at her. "Will he act on it?"

I just blinked. "Huh?"

"Will he act on the need for the ladies? You know him, so you should know the answer."

Silence stretched between us, the only sounds being that of Davis's soft sleeping. As my eyes started to cloud with tears, I slowly shook my head. "No, he wouldn't. He loves me."

She nodded, her lips curving. "And do you love him?"

I swallowed hard. "I do."

"Okay, then what's wrong? What are you thinking?"

I shrugged. "I'm embarrassed by how things played out, and I'm scared that even though I think he won't hurt me, and that he loves me, he will hurt me. He's all about these promises, and I hate promises—"

"With Jesse," she supplied. "You hate the promises that Jesse made. You know you can't make this guy pay for Jesse's mistakes, don't you?"

When my tears started to fall, it was no longer because of everything that was happening with Gus. That was part of it, but it was mainly because my mom was finally being my mom again. I had waited for this for so long. Covering my face with my hands, I slowly nodded, and when I felt her arms around me, I leaned into her.

"Bocephus, baby, you haven't dated anyone in years, haven't even talked about anyone, but now you are. You talk about him, and you get this look in your eyes. Baby, that has to mean something."

"It does," I whispered. "It really does."

"Good. Baby, you have to live your life and love it. If this man helps you live and loves you, why fight, baby?"

"Because I'm an idiot?"

She laughed against my ear as she kissed my temple. "Then stop being an idiot."

"Easier said than done," I laughed, and she kissed my cheek before holding my face.

"I love you, baby, and I want you to be happy."

"I do too," I said as my tears continued to fall. "I love you, Mom."

She smiled widely at me before kissing me hard on the cheek just as my phone went off. Pulling away, we both looked down at it, and I saw that it was in fact from Gus, and there was a lot.

"Is that him?"

I nodded. "Yeah. Gus. His name is Gus."

She smiled. "Answer him."

She patted my face, and then she was gone as I lifted my phone, opening the message.

Gus: *This is going to be long, so get comfortable. When you left last night, I sat there for a moment, waiting for the relief to come. Like, finally, I was out of this relationship, I could go back to my old ways, and I would be awesome. But relief didn't come. I was just miserable. I didn't know what to do, I didn't how to make you answer me or anything. I felt like I was dying. So I stayed up most of the night trying to figure out what to do, and I came up with nothing, because no matter what I do, no matter what I say, it won't matter if you don't want me. The funny thing is, I really thought you did. I seriously thought we were solid. Like right now, I'm standing in a hall waiting for the team doctors to look at me, and all I want is to come to you and tell you that I have a spot here with the Tornadoes. I got it. And I'm excited and I'm ready, but I wish like hell you were here with me. I want to kiss you, I want to share this with you, because, Bo, I love you. Don't you get that? I love you and only you. Yeah, I know you hate promises, they're stupid, or whatever you called them. The thing is, when I was eight years old, I watched my dad promise my mom he would never hurt her. He would never leave her. And he promised he'd love her until he was dead in the ground. He's kept those promises and even made more. And he's kept them all. I want to be that man. I want to be that man for you. I want to give you a new standard. I don't want you to look at promises or hockey players and think they're shit. Well, actually, you can think that about anyone else except me. You have to like me, but you get what I'm saying? This would be so much easier on the phone, but if this is how it has to be, fine. Because I promise I'll never leave you unless you send me away. I promise to support you even when you don't support yourself. And I promise to give all the orgasms you could ever want or need. But most of all, I'll always want you, and I love you. Even when you don't want me. So call me. I want to see you.*

I covered my mouth and closed my eyes as the sobs raked through me. His words, his promises, everything just shattered me. He rattled me. He was full of surprises, and it honestly blew me away. I thought he was this one-dimensional guy, but he was so much more.

And I wanted it all.

All of him.

As I stared at my phone, a goofy grin moved across my face.

How in the world was I supposed to say anything but yes to a text message like that?

CHAPTER THIRTY-FOUR

GUS

"Nothing is broken."

I wanted to throw my hands up, but I knew that might hurt, so I didn't. Instead, I just flashed him a grin. "So, I'm good?"

"Yeah, we'll freeze you up before the game tomorrow, but you'll stay tender for a while. As long as you want to play, I'm not going to stop you, unless, of course, something changes."

I was going to like this doctor a lot. "Great. So, really, I'm fine?"

"Yeah, solid. It was awesome to meet you. Hope I don't see you again."

I shook his hand. "Me too, brother. Thanks."

Taking in a deep and painful breath, I felt pretty good other than the fact that my phone hadn't gone off. Bo was still radio silent, and it was honestly killing me. But then my phone started to ring, and I almost dropped it trying to answer it.

Instead of Bo, it was Max.

"Max, what's up?"

"Dude, you haven't called me, and I've been calling you."

"I'm sorry, sweetheart, but I told you, I've moved on," I somehow teased, even though I didn't want to.

Max did laugh a bit though. "Shut it, asshole. Listen, I got traded."

"No shit," I said, stopping in the hall. "Where?"

"New York."

"Fuck yeah! Dude, that's awesome!"

"Yeah, I'm leaving as soon as possible."

"Dude, I'm so happy for you. You got a spot?"

"Yeah, can you believe it?"

"I can!"

"Thanks, man. Listen, Jessica is gonna meet me up there. I don't think I'll get to say goodbye though."

I scoffed at his bromancing way, but then, we had become more than friends. Brothers, actually. "Dude, it's fine. I was about to call you. I got the spot on the Tornadoes!"

"Oh, thank God! That's awesome, man," he gushed, and I smiled.

"Yeah, so we'll play each other, and I'll take you and Jessica out. Since, of course, I make more money than you."

He laughed. "I'm gonna miss you, man. Make sure you bring Bo with you."

The smile dropped from my face. Since I hadn't heard from her after laying my heart out, I was pretty sure that meant it was over. Which fucking sucked.

"Hey, I'm dropping Sweetie off with Lizzy. She'll keep her until you can come get her," he added.

"Cool," I said, because I wasn't about to ruin his mood. He didn't need to know about the shit with Bo. Hell, I didn't even really know what the shit was. Except that I was hurting everywhere. "So, good luck!"

"Thanks, man. You too."

Hanging up, I exhaled hard and couldn't believe how things were changing so fast. Max and I had been buddies for the last year. Both of us worked our asses off, and finally, we were getting somewhere. I looked at my phone and started to text Bo. I had to tell her, but I paused when I saw that she had read my message.

Yet, she hadn't answered my last text.

"Damn it," I moaned, leaning into the door as my hand fell to my side. Maybe I should just go to her mom's house, try to talk to her. But what was the point? She'd probably just ignore me like she was now.

Fuck, what a load of bullshit.

Tucking my phone into my pocket, I decided to go to the bar. Maybe my dad would come down to the hotel bar with me so we could discuss how shitty women were. I needed a drink, and I needed to forget that my first ever girlfriend just blew me off like I was nothing. Man, that hurt.

I just didn't get it, though. I had told her everything I was feeling. Wasn't that enough?

Shaking my head, I headed out of the compound just as my phone started to ring.

It was my mom.

"Hey, I was about to call you—"

"Gus!" she cried out, and everything went tight.

"Mom? What's wrong?"

"Dad and I were getting ready to catch a cab to go shopping when we saw Bo crossing the street! She got hit by a car!"

"What?" I almost cried, my heart pounding in my chest.

"Is she okay?"

"I don't know. They just got her in the ambulance and are taking her to the ER."

I didn't even wait for more. I hung up, and then I was running.

Because even though she didn't like them, I had made a promise to her.

And I would never break that.

◆ ◆ ◆ ◆

When I got to the ER, it was dead. There was no one in there, unlike when I'd ended up there in Malibu. So, thankfully, it was easy to find the nurses' desk.

"I'm looking for Bocephus St. James."

The older lady glanced up at me and then paused before she looked me up and down. If I wasn't stricken with worry about Bo, I would have been offended at having been checked out like a piece of chocolate cake. Okay, I probably wouldn't have been offended, but either way, I was shaking I was so worried.

"Family member?"

"Boyfriend," I answered. "I'm her boyfriend. Gus Persson."

"Ah yes, she did have your name down." I had to keep myself from fist pumping. Not only would it have hurt, but also I was pretty sure that would have been pathetic. "She's behind curtain six. I'll open the doors for you."

"Is she okay?"

"You'll have to see for yourself, Mr. Persson."

Well, that wasn't promising.

Rushing from her desk, I ran through the doors she had opened and realized that I was sweating profusely. My heart was going insane in my chest, and I felt like I couldn't breathe. What if her ankle was really broken this time? What if she was paralyzed? Shit, what if she was brain dead!

When I got to the hall that held all the waiting rooms with the curtains giving everyone privacy, I sped down it, counting the curtains, until I got to six.

Staring at the number, I looked around at all the open curtains, but no one was in them. I didn't see a doctor. I didn't see anyone, but I heard the beeping of a machine behind the curtain. Reaching out to pull it open, my hand was shaking so damn bad I almost didn't want to open it. I didn't want to see her, hurt and broken, and not be able to tell her that she was my world.

"Grow a sack, Bus," I whispered to myself before pulling the curtain open.

To my surprise, Bo wasn't in the bed. She was standing beside it in a pair of leggings and a long shirt that was tied at the side. Her hair was up in her trusty bun, and she was wearing some makeup. She did have her boot on, but other than that, she didn't look like a car had hit her.

A small smile curved her lips as she slowly shrugged. She was holding a piece of paper, but I was too freaked out to read it. "Gus—"

"Wait," I said, holding my hand up. "Are you okay?"

She looked around, and I did the same. The room was a standard room, but it was full of candles, and then on the bed was a box of pizza and some beer. Wasn't sure how she got that in here since they wouldn't let us bring in beer in Malibu, but then maybe the rules were different here. Not that that mattered, since she was supposed to have been hit by a car!

"Yeah, I'm fine. We always said we should have date night here—"

I held my hand up again, stopping her. "My mom told me you got hit by a car."

Her jaw dropped, and then she started to sputter with laughter. "What! I told her to tell you I twisted my ankle again!"

I inhaled hard, running my hands down my face. "I'm going to kill her."

"You guys have a really funny relationship."

"Yeah, they're basically children and I'm the adult."

Bo scoffed at that. "I mean, I wouldn't go that far."

I tucked my hands into my pockets and looked up at her. She looked back at me, her cheeks full of color as she chewed on her lip. I wanted to close the distance between us, kiss away all the lip gloss she wore, but I wasn't sure what was going on here.

But that didn't matter, because without thinking, I reached for her, pulling her hard to me before crashing my lips to hers. She kissed me back with just as much need as her fingers trailed up the back of my neck into my hair. Squeezing her in my arms, I heard the crunch of the paper she was holding, but I didn't care because I wanted to cry out in elation. I parted only slightly and whispered, "I texted you."

"I know," she whispered back, moving her hands down my face, her thumbs resting against my lips. "I wanted to answer back, but I couldn't do it over the phone. I wanted to do it in person."

Swallowing hard, I held her gaze. "So what did you want to say?"

"That I was sorry," she said as an exhale. "That I was an idiot, and that I can't keep trying to make you pay for the pain that Jesse brought me. You aren't him, and I knew that from the beginning, which is why I stopped hating you so quickly."

My face broke into a grin. "You never hated me."

She eyed me. "I did." Moving my hands up her back and into her hair, I searched her gaze. She was just so beautiful. "But, um, I was talking to my mom today, and she made a good point, that I'm dragging around my past as if it's chained to me. I don't want to do that anymore. I don't want to think of my past. I only want to live in the now, with you."

I pressed my forehead to hers. "That's all I want."

"I don't know what is going to happen."

"It doesn't matter, because the thing is, Bo, I'll never finish loving you. It just keeps going on and on. I've finished a lot of things. A period during a game, a goal, and plenty of women that I shouldn't really be bringing up, but oh well, it's part of my point. With you it's constant and I can't... I just can't finish. And all I want is for you to love me back and for us to be happy. The future will fall into place as long as we have each other."

She sighed softly as she gazed up at me. She wiggled her arms up, and I pulled back some so she could hold up her piece of paper.

I want to make promises with you.

Everything inside of me just blew up as I met her gaze

again.

"I didn't want this. I really didn't, you know I didn't, but it just seems like we're supposed to happen. I have never made anyone a promise because of what happened, but now, I want to make the same promises you made to me. Because I don't want anything other than to be with you."

"Me too. Fuck, baby, me too," I demanded, cupping her face. "Listen, I want you to move here with me. I really do, but if you want to finish school, that's fine. We'll make it work because we won't settle for anything el—"

"I want to move with you," she said, cutting me off. "I'll transfer, or whatever, I'll make it work. I want to be wherever you are. And Sweetie. I can't forget Sweetie."

"Really?" I asked, and I felt the tears burning my eyes. Every single dream I'd had since the moment I met her was coming true. "You really want that?"

"I do, as long as you want it."

"You're damn right I do," I said before taking her mouth with mine. As I drew out the kisses, she melted against me, and I wanted nothing more than to spend my days doing just this. Being with her. Loving her.

She was what happiness felt like.

Pulling back, I moved my fingers along her temple, into her hair, as she said, "I can't promise that I won't bring up my past again."

"That's fine." I pressed my nose to hers. "I can't promise I won't annoy the fuck out of you."

"You will, and I'll hold out on sex."

"Seems fair."

"I thought so."

We shared a smile. "But something I can promise, there will always be a seat for you at all my games."

She beamed up at me. "I'll be there, as long as I get to come home with you."

"Done deal," I answered as our gazes burned together. We shared a smile, and my eyes slowly drifted shut as I wrapped my arms around her neck and hers came around my torso. "One more thing."

"Yeah?"

"I promise I'll love you. For the rest of our lives."

"Good, 'cause I can promise the same thing."

"Can't say it, huh?"

She giggled against my lips. "Gus."

"Bocephus Jane St. James?"

She didn't even glare. She kept smiling as she held me in her arms. "I love you too." She let out a long breath. "I love you so damn much."

Oh, those words. Just four simple little words that basically demolished my world within seconds. I thought hearing my name fall from her lips was the best sound in the world. Boy, was I wrong. I knew from this moment on, I'd never be the same.

Never.

What more could I ask for? Well, maybe fewer trips to the ER, but then again, I fell madly, deeply, insanely in love with Bo there.

So yeah, I wouldn't ask for that. Instead, I'd kiss her again. Because I was Bo's.

And she was mine.

And I was cocky enough to know that life was going to be great.

EXCERPT FROM
MISADVENTURES WITH THE BOSS

My Netflix account was judging me.

At least that was how it felt every time I had to insist *Yes, Netflix, I am still watching* Absolutely Fabulous, *thank you very much.* I imagined it asking even more invasive questions—questions my sister would ask if she were here.

Are you sure you want to keep watching?

Didn't you move to the city for all the exciting nightlife?

And, more importantly—*what kind of twenty-something spends their evening watching so many old sitcoms?*

I grabbed the throw pillow beside me, tucked it under my chin, and snuggled it close to my chest, ignoring the clunk of my phone as it tumbled to the floor. It wasn't like anyone was going to call and ask me to hang out anyway. I was so new to the city that I was still surrounded by boxes that desperately needed to be unpacked.

But not tonight. Tonight I was determined to sit like a stubborn bump on a lazy log and do nothing.

Raising the remote, I turned up the volume as the theme song faded and the show began. But just as the dialogue was really starting to heat up, my phone broke into the jazzy, happy tone I'd selected for one caller in particular—my sister.

Think of the devil.

I let it play on a bit, debating whether to answer. I then reached for the floor, snagged my phone from the carpet, and pressed it to my face.

"Hello?" I said, waiting for Hailey's chipper voice to fill the speaker.

"Piper," she deadpanned.

"What?" I asked, already feeling defensive and biting back a groan.

First mistake?

Answering the phone.

"Where are you right now? I don't hear anything going on behind you. No music. No chatter. Tell me at least you're at some gallery looking at glorious paintings and sipping champagne," she demanded.

If things were quiet on my end, the same could definitely not be said for hers. As usual, bass-filled music blared behind her voice, getting softer as she moved through whichever bar was the flavor of the week. There were a lot of things a person could say about Hailey, but nobody could ever accuse her of not knowing her way around a party. To be perfectly honest, I was shocked I didn't hear people chanting her name in the distance, begging her to join them for another shot.

She was like a people magnet, and I was...well, what's the opposite of a people magnet?

Whatever the answer is, that's me.

"I'm home." I stared at the stack of brown cardboard boxes and forced a white lie from my lips because the truth was just too depressing to say. "Unpacking. And can you go outside or something? The music wherever you are is so loud."

"Right." I could practically hear her roll her eyes, but in a matter of minutes, the music had dimmed to practically nothing. "Why aren't you out?"

"Who am I going to go out with?"

"I don't know. You just go out. Find people along the way."

I sighed. "I'm not like you. I don't just enter a room and have people flock to me."

"But aren't you lonely?"

I bit my cheek. "I never said I wasn't."

"So what are you going to do? Just sit around your apartment and hope friends magically appear?"

"I just got a new job. I'll meet people there when I start."

Hailey blew out a frustrated sigh. "This isn't like college or high school. You can't just expect to hang with the people you see all day. We're in the modern age, Pipes. You've gotta throw yourself into it. Take risks. Get wild."

"What, like, join a chat room or something?"

"No, you weirdo. Use an app. All the dating sites have find-a-friend features," she replied, matter-of-fact.

"Well, ideally I wouldn't find my friends where people are also trying to get into my pants," I said primly.

"And why not? I'm willing to bet nobody has gotten into your sensible slacks in a good long while, either," my sister said with a snort.

"Hailey," I warned, but she pressed on.

"Come *on*, everybody's doing it," Hailey said. "What could it hurt?"

My pride?

I should have said it aloud, of course, but just like everyone else, I had fallen under the magic spell that Hailey cast on everyone she met. I wanted to please her—to let her have her way. She was just so cool. So everything I wasn't.

"Exactly," Hailey said into the silence. "Even you can't come up with a reason not to. I'm putting you on speaker so I can make you an account right now." There was the sound of fumbling, and then my sister's voice came back over the line again. "Okay, ready. You still have the same email address?"

Sucked into the whirlwind that was Hailey and at a loss to come up with a reason why I shouldn't do this, I nodded, and then catching myself, I said, "Uh, yeah. Same one."

"Great. Now we need to come up with a username for you."

"How about Piper Daniels? My name," I said dryly.

"Do you even internet?" Hailey said with a groan. "No, I think not. We don't need stalkers tracking you down and trying to make dresses out of your skin."

I winced and rubbed at my temple with my fingertip. "If you're trying to convince me this is a good idea, you're not doing a great job."

Frankly, all of this was giving me a tension headache. I glanced longingly at the TV as she continued.

"Relax. We'll root out the weirdos. Now focus. We need a screen name. Think something cute. Something that speaks to who you are as a person."

I paused, but all I could come up with was Piper Longstocking. Between my freckles and my dark-red hair, it was a nickname that had come all too easy to the less-creative relatives in my family. I suggested this to my sister, and as expected, she scoffed.

"Jesus. God, no. Nothing about that screams sexy to me."

"I'm not trying to scream sexy. I'm trying to find friends," I reminded her.

"Well, we're keeping our options open," she hedged in a way that made the hairs on the back of my neck stand up. "Besides, there's going to be a picture of you on the profile. I used that one from cousin Anna's wedding."

"The one where I'm sneezing?" I hissed, mortified.

"No. What do you take me for, woman? There's another one. You look cute, trust me. Now, let's focus this name on something you like to do or something about you. You're all organized, right? What about something to do with that?"

"Planning Piper?" I suggested.

"I don't like it. We need to make it sexier."

"Hail—"

"I've got it. Okay. Typed and saved. Can't change it now."

"I'm afraid to ask," I groaned.

"Oh, it's nothing bad. Just, you know, roll with the punches."

"And what punches am I rolling with?"

She mumbled at first, so low that I couldn't hear her.

"What was that?" I asked.

"Fantasy Girl 29," she said more clearly.

"What?" I yelped. "Are you serious? What kind of person is looking to be friends with someone who names herself Fantasy Girl 29?"

"What? You love fantasy stuff. You're all into, like, *Game of Thrones* and *Lord of the Rings*, so I thought—"

"That is not how people are going to read that, Hail."

"Oh well. What's done is done," she said in a rush. "Now we just need to answer some questions. You're a 29-year-old female with a bangin' bod, and you're looking for friendship, long- and short-term relationships, and casual sex."

Panic shot through me, and I let out a squeak. "I am not looking for—"

"Aren't you?" Hailey cut in. "Be honest with me for just a second here. What would it really hurt for you to get a good, rough bone in every now and again? It's been ages since you and Tommy broke up, and I seriously doubt you found yourself a fuck boy to get over it, so—"

I wrinkled my nose. "No, I moved to a new city to start fresh and get away from him. Now come on, don't..."

"Too late. Already done," Hailey chirped. "No going back now."

I pinched my nose between two fingers. "Right. Of course not."

"Now let's answer some questions. You drink occasionally, and you don't smoke. Those are easy. You're an animal person."

"I'm allergic to cats," I said.

"But you like them. Good enough."

"Why do I get the feeling I should hang up and just let

you do whatever you're going to do?"

"Come on, don't be like that," she pleaded in that sweet voice that made me want to hand her the moon on a platter. "Now let's get to the real questions, shall we? Okay, if you were going to have one romantic night anywhere in the world, where would you choose?"

I thought hard. Some girls would say Paris. Others would say a picnic on the edge of a lake.

Me? I glanced at my paused TV and said, "In my apartment. Homemade dinner and some movies. Perfect night."

Hailey groaned. "I'll never understand how we came from the same people's loins, but I'm writing it down because I love you, and surely there is someone out there who will too. Okay, next one. On a scale of one to ten, how adventurous are you?"

"One," I said.

"Five, then," Hailey corrected. "Nobody says one. They'll think you cower in your apartment like a hermit, afraid to leave the house."

"That's kind of what I do."

"But people don't need to know that."

And so it went. Over and over again—for roughly a million questions—Hailey asked me about myself and then corrected me to make me more palatable to other people. When at last we'd finished, she clicked into my profile and let out a contented sigh.

"Okay, here's your description. Hey there! I'm Piper, and I'm looking for like-minded people to hang out with as

I'm new to the city. My interests include Netflix, a good glass of wine, board games, and snuggly couches," Hailey said.

"Good enough," I said, compromising because it was the best I was going to get from her at this point.

"Great," she said, smacking her lips with satisfaction. "Ooh, lookie here! You've already got a match."

"What?" My stomach kicked up a team of butterflies. "Are you serious?"

"Dead. Oh, wow," Hailey cooed. "He's sexy."

"I'm not looking for sexy," I reminded her.

"Oh, you're *definitely* looking for this kind of sexy. Everyone wants this kind of sexy. Holy cow."

"How do you know he's not going to make a wig out of my skin or whatever you said?" I reminded her, trying not to let the panic set in.

"Oh, relax. You can keep me on speed dial through your whole date."

"Date?" I asked.

"It's tomorrow night at the Florentine Inn. That place is nice, so wear a dress," she chirped.

"What the hell, Hail?" I said, my palms going clammy even at the thought.

"Don't worry, you don't have to thank me just yet."

"Cancel it," I shot back. "Cancel it right now."

"No. You need to get out there, and this is the only way you're ever going to do it. I'm just giving you a gentle shove, sis," Hailey insisted.

It felt more like a knife in my back. Everything in me wanted to fight her on this. Everything except this one, teeny tiny part of me that feared she was right—and I was terrified to spend the rest of my life alone. Of sitting inside this apartment with no one to talk to and nothing to do and, worse, getting more comfortable with it day by day until the only people I saw were workmates and Thai food delivery guys. That part had me considering it. Just this one time.

"Well, tell me something about him, at least," I grumbled.

"Nope. You have to go into this with an open mind, and at least this way, I know you will."

For a female, the size of my sister's balls never failed to astonish me. "You're evil," I said.

"Yep, but you are going to like this guy and end up thanking me. I can feel it. Now I've gotta go. When I left, some chick was talking about riding the mechanical bull, and I'm pretty sure it's about to get hilarious in there. Love you."

She hung up, and I glared at my phone for a long moment before setting it on the coffee table in front of me and staring at the TV.

I couldn't remember the last time I'd been on a first date—maybe not since college. I'd thought, way back when, that Tommy and I were going to make it, that we'd get married. But no. He got promoted to Head Douchebag or whatever his title was at some real-estate firm, and he left me in the dust. And then, with his face plastered on every billboard in town to promote the firm, I couldn't get away from the guy.

I'd needed a fresh start—something new. Different. So

I came here.

And I've been wallowing and watching Netflix ever since. Though, to be fair, it had only been three days.

Placing my hands just outside my thighs, I propelled myself from the couch and made my way toward the calendar hanging from my fridge. Monday was labelled with bright-green ink—my first day at my new job. And tomorrow?

Tomorrow was a day for pink. The color of romance.

I picked a pen from a little cup near the fridge, wrote the time and place of my date on the calendar, and then stood back and smiled. Hailey could be right. This could be my one chance to get back on the wagon and spend my Friday nights somewhere other than lounging on my couch alone.

And she was right about one other thing too.

It had been a long, long time since I'd felt the warmth of a man's skin against me. And the fact that I didn't know a thing about this guy? Well, that made it all the more terrifying...but also kind of exciting.

The best part? If it didn't work out, I'd never have to see him again. Maybe Hailey had really come up with the perfect plan this time.

This story continues in Misadventures with the Boss!

ACKNOWLEDGMENTS

I'm going to try not to forget everyone. I'm so awful at these things.

First, I want to thank my amazing family, Michael, Mikey, Alyssa, and Gaston. Everything I do, I do it for y'all. I love you all, so damn much, and nothing will ever change that. To the rest of my family, I love you.

Then my tribe, Bobbie Jo, Kristen, and Nortis. These women are my rocks. They believe in me when I don't believe in myself.

To my life manager, Lisa Holleta. Everyone knows I can't do life without you. You truly have my best interest in mind and I truly appreciate that. It's amazing to be able to trust someone so completely and know they have you. I will always love you, Holletta. Thank you for all you do.

When I started in this business, God gave me women to help me make sure to give the best book I can, my betas, Laurie, Heather, Jessica, Althea, Franci, Susie, and Nicole. They are the best, I love y'all.

To Chelle Bliss. I love you girl. Really. I couldn't do a lot of my work life without you.

To my editing team: Scott and Jeanne. Thank you so much for dealing with all this crazy. I know it hasn't been easy but I am blessed to have y'all in my life. Thank you so much for all you've done. I look forward to our future together.

To Meredith Wild and her amazing husband, thank you for being so kind. For always believing in me and for just being effing awesome.

To my Misadventures sisters, y'all are amazing. Thank you for being there for me when I needed someone to pick me up. I love you all.

To the whole Misadventures team, thank you. Thank you so much for being the best team a girl could get.

And last, but definitely not least, David Grishman. I don't think there are enough words to truly thank you for what you've done for me. You believed in some crazy, country, hockey nut and gave her her dream. I offered you a kidney and while I'm glad you didn't take it, I honestly wish I could figure out a way to thank you. I look forward to our future together and I can honestly say I've never been happier to be with such an amazing publishing house. Thank you. Thank you so very much.

MORE MISADVENTURES

VISIT MISADVENTURES.COM
FOR MORE INFORMATION!

MORE MISADVENTURES